In The Eye Of The Beholder

A Novel of the
Phantom of the Opera

Sharon E. Cathcart

In The Eye Of The Beholder
A Novel of the Phantom of the Opera
By Sharon E. Cathcart

©2009 by Sharon E. Cathcart

All rights reserved.
This book or parts thereof may not be reproduced in any form, stored in a retrieval system, or transmitted in any form by any means without prior written permission of the authors, except as provided by United States of America copyright law.

Cover Design/All Artwork: James Courtney

Published by: TreasureLine Publishing
www.OneStopPublisher.com

ISBN: 1-61752-000-4
EAN-13: 978-1-61752-000-6

Printed in the United States of America.

First paperback edition: UK ISBN is 978-0-9561884-7-2
(Turner Maxwell Books, 2009)
eBook: 978-1-4523-0030-6 (Smashwords, 2009)

www.TreasureLineBooks.com

Author's Note

This is a work of fiction. While historical persons do appear within the text, all events are of my own imagination.

During the 19th century, and for nearly the first half of the 20th century, French women were not allowed to vote, nor to have a bank account or passport/traveling papers without express written permission of a father or husband. They had no property rights, not even to their own clothing and jewelry. They had no legal status whatsoever outside of being a daughter or a wife. These facts inform much of Claire Delacroix's background, and her intellectual rebellion against her place in "proper society."

Everyone I have spoken to has his or her own vision of Erik, the Phantom of the Opera. My vision is an amalgam of persons known to and/or admired by me. To that end, I thank my husband Jeffrey Cathcart, my dear friend Tom Westlake, and actors Gerard Butler and Earl Carpenter for inspiration. I am also grateful to Paddy Doyle Cathcart, who became Pierre in these pages.

CHAPTER 1

Paris, France
March, 1889

"Who did this to her?"

My eyes scanned the silent faces of the stable hands as I laid my hand on Josephine's steaming neck, listening to the black mare suck hard to get a breath of air. Her knees were bloody. All eyes were downcast under my ire.

I had heard the commotion as the horse was brought back to the stables at the Opera Garnier, where I was an equestrienne trainer and performer. Horses were frequently used in the operas and Josephine was my gentlest mare, a beautiful Dutch Friesian. She was poetry in motion, and I could guide her with nothing more than a wide ribbon around her neck. She and I had a scene in Meyerbeer's "Prophete" in which we did just that, the mare's steps performing a powerful ballet guided solely by my legs and the ribbon.

Again I glared at the men, stalking the circle around my winded, sweating horse. I tapped my riding crop against my green-topped boots, which just showed under my sturdy, tan twill divided riding skirt. My blue eyes blazed angrily at each of them and my chestnut braid flapped against my black blouse as I paced.

"Who did this to her," I demanded again.

I caught a muttering toward the back, and turned toward the sound. One of the performers twisted his hat in his hands.

"Mademoiselle Claire, it was me," said Giraud, the chief hand.

"I was bragging on Josephine to some friends at the tavern, that you could ride her with nothing but a ribbon around her neck. I took her to show them, and they challenged me to a race. I tried her over a jump, and she couldn't take it. She would have won." His gaze on me grew defiant. "I lost twenty sous."

"You fool," I cried. "Josephine is not a hunter. She was trained for *haute ecole*. And now she will not be able to perform tonight." I was close to tears listening to the poor mare's labored breath, her head dropped to her ruined knees. "Messieurs Dupin and Richard will not be happy about this."

"You could ride Pierrot," suggested my cousin Francois, the troupe leader. "He's almost ready."

Ah yes, Pierrot: the far more fractious black Andalusian. Beautiful, fiery and, as Francois indicated, almost ready. I could do the scene with a bridle, I supposed.

"Francois, send to Dupin and Richard and let them know that Josephine is injured, and that the horse scene will be done differently as a result. I will look to Josephine. You must look to Pierrot." My cousin nodded his assent and went to take care of the horse. "As for the rest of you, go on about your business."

I looked at the watch pinned to my blouse and realized that there would, no doubt, be another black-edged note waiting for me this evening since I was now late in caring for Cesare. However, my Josephine came first.

As I laved Josephine's knees with cool water prior to preparing a poultice, I remembered the first note.

"Mademoiselle Delacroix, I have seen your kindness and

expertise with the horses. I have a horse, Cesare, for whom your services are required. You will groom him promptly at five o'clock each evening, while the hands from the stables are caring for your own animals. You will provide his evening feed of the same treacle and grain formulation you provide to your own horses. You will find him in a stall on the fifth basement of the opera. Come alone, and do not dare to tell others of this mission. O.G."

Like so many involved in the Opera Garnier, I knew the legend of the so-called Opera Ghost and his linkage to the Vicomte and Comtesse de Chagny: how the Phantom had loved and trained Christine Daae, a soubrette. He saw to it that she came out of the chorus to become a prima donna. She then unmasked him onstage.

I had no idea that he still lived until I received that note. It had been almost a year since the incidents in question, after all. Nevertheless, I could not in good conscience fail to at least examine Cesare for myself, to see what his needs were -- if, in fact, this horse existed and it was not another stable hand joke.

I wrapped Josephine's knees in a poultice and walked her around the yard to cool her. There had been many stable hand "pranks" and "jokes" since I came to the Opera Garnier eight months ago with Francois and his equestrian troupe. I resisted all advances despite my loneliness, which clearly annoyed the men around me. Especially Giraud, who had set his cap for me. Thus, any opportunity to vex me was taken. I cast my memory back, even as I spoke soothingly to the mare.

I had indeed found a horse in a stall in the fifth basement. Cesare was a beautiful pale gray Lipizzan, nearly white, with gentle ground manners. He stood still while being brushed and curried, and nuzzled me whenever he saw me. The horse was in the peak of health and ridden regularly. A pouch containing ten francs was always left in the horse's stall; I was paid for my extra work. I was grateful for the extra money, for my pay envelope was not a large one.

After an hour of walking Josephine, I returned her to her stall with a warm mash. I covered her in a rug and then hurried to the fifth basement stall. As usual, Cesare was there; of course, there was also a note, a black-edged card whose envelope was sealed with a red death's head in wax.

"Mademoiselle Delacroix, I know what happened to Josephine. Your gentleness with her was noted. Please care for Cesare as usual. O.G."

I put the note in my skirt pocket and went about my usual routine with Cesare. I leaned against his warm flank as I brushed him, wondering what I would do about Giraud. I hadn't the authority to dismiss him, but I surely wished I could. I sighed, and finished grooming the horse. Since I had begun to care for the handsome animal, I braided his mane and tail as the last bit of my routine; when the braids were let down, the hair rippled and shimmered. I had no doubt that whoever rode the fine animal made quite a picture.

I completed my tasks and returned to my chambers to prepare for the night's performance. Overhead, I heard a beautiful male voice singing. This was not the first time: probably one of the chorus boys practicing in the echoing halls. It made no difference to me who was singing; it was a soothing sound, and enticing at the same time.

The water boys had already brought a hot tub to my room. I undressed and settled into the bath, using rose-scented soap that I purchased in a small shop nearby. After bathing, I stepped out of the tub, dried myself, and dressed in my diaphanous green costume for the performance. I also wore black velvet boots with soft soles; the boots blended in with Josephine's coat. I was tempted to wear my regular riding boots with Pierrot and use the saddle with the stirrups attached for a change. The stallion was young and far more distractible. However, a certain element of professional pride made me decide against it. I would use the ribbons and the flat *haute ecole* saddle, just as I did with Josephine. If I lacked confidence in myself or the horse, he would sense it and this would not help matters.

I stood before the pier glass and tightened my riding corset of pale green silk. My figure was more lush than the current fashion dictated; I had full breasts and hips, albeit with a small waist. In an age that preferred the willowy silhouette, I was an anachronism. I was also diminutive in height, topping five feet tall by just an inch. The most dramatic moment of my performance was when I dismounted, demonstrating how much smaller I was than the horse and, with a simple gesture, had her tower beside me on her hind legs before returning to a stand and then bending one leg to bow.

I sighed as I brushed out my hair from its practical braid. My hair was not long, just to my shoulder blades, but the braid kept it out of my face when I was working with the horses. For performances, I wore it down; I was supposed to be some sort of a sylph with magical powers over the beasts. I finished my toilette by making up my face for the stage. The footlights required extra enhancements so that the performer's face could be seen, but I wanted the audience to focus on the horse.

As I turned away from the glass, I noticed the rose. Its long stem was wrapped in black silk ribbon. I had never received flowers in my room; that was always for the chorus girls or singers. I was merely the horse woman and not sought after by admirers, whom I would only have discouraged anyway. Perhaps Francois had left it for me; he knew I loved the scent. My cousin and I were not close, but he made such kind gestures from time to time.

I glanced at the clock: it was nearly time for me to be in the stable to warm up the horse prior to our appearance. I hurried down the short flight of stairs, wanting to take the extra time with Pierrot.

This was not the life I had envisioned for myself.

CHAPTER 2

Baincthuin, France
1857-1888

My father, Michel Delacroix, left the Camargue, in the South of France, under the cloud of scandal. Like many of the Camargois, he had a gift for horsemanship: a gift he had passed on to me. He worked on one of the Camargois cattle ranches, and his handsome face, dancing blue eyes and dark hair caught the attention of the landholder's daughter.

My mother, Marie-Louise Lunel, possessed an independent streak. The blonde beauty spent more and more time around the horse barns, and soon she and the charming Michel decided to wed. Her father would hear none of it and, when the two ultimately eloped, cut her off. She and my father left the Camargue and traveled all the way to Baincthuin to make their home.

My father trained horses for others and made wine from grapes that grew in a little arbor behind the modest house. My mother, who had been born to a life of leisure, worked for a milliner. According to my father, they were very happy. I never knew my mother; she died giving birth to me.

My father, in many ways, reared me as though I were a son. He taught me how to gentle a horse rather than breaking its spirit. He taught me how to ride, as well as how to read and write. When I was old enough, I attended the village school house. Eventually, as happened with the daughters of wealthier families, he sent me to

Switzerland for boarding school.

I loved Zurich, with its cosmopolitan air. I made friends with young ladies from many different countries and could converse passably in German, Italian and English by the time I returned to Baincthuin.

By the same token, I loved the house in Baincthuin, with its stone walls and tiled floors. There were fireplaces for warmth in winter, and large windows to allow the breezes in during the summer. In the back area of the property were pastures, a large wooden barn, and the grape arbor.

There was no cotillion or coming-out for me. My father spent a great deal of money on my education, and there was not much left for such fripperies. As other young ladies around me married, I was still single well into my twenties. I had no doubt that I would be the much-joked about old maid of Baincthuin, tending my horses. I was resigned to remaining on the proverbial shelf.

I was twenty-nine years old when Philippe Andreux came to Baincthuin. It was June of 1887.

Philippe sought my father's advice on winemaking. He had inherited a significant sum of money and decided to become a gentleman vintner. So, he left Paris for Baincthuin, which had a reputation as a town where fine wines were made. He could have chosen the Alsace, Bordeaux or any other area, but he came to our village.

The first time I met Philippe, I was riding Josephine back to the house. I was wearing breeches and shirt, with my hair pulled back in a braid. I alighted at the front of the house near a carriage that I did not recognize.

"Mademoiselle?"

A voice that I likewise did not recognize, and then a golden Apollo emerged from the carriage.

"I seek Michel Delacroix. Where might I find him? I have rapped at the door and no one has answered."

"My father will no doubt be in the back," I responded, trying to keep from gaping at this most handsome creature. "I will take you." I pulled Josephine's reins over her head and walked her toward the barn and grape arbors. "Please come with me."

"I am Philippe Andreux," he said. "And you are?"

"Claire Delacroix. I am honored to make your acquaintance."

"Mademoiselle Delacroix, do you not fear to scandalize the countryside in your breeches?" There was a touch of humor in the question.

"Monsieur, if this is all that it takes to scandalize the countryside, then I suggest that those in the countryside see more of the world." I looked at him sidelong, with just a hint of a smile.

Philippe burst into laughter then. "Are all of the women in Baincthuin like you?"

"I suggest, monsieur, that you meet all of the women in Baincthuin and find out." Philippe's laughter at my sally was infectious, and I found myself laughing as well.

Philippe began courting me not long after that first meeting. He told me that he preferred my "originality" to the simpering behavior of the Parisian women. At the same time, he preferred my education to that of the Baincthuinoise ladies. I read constantly, and was always prepared to discuss the latest books. I loved to hear Philippe's tales of life in Paris and hoped to go there one day.

Still, I was astonished when Philippe sought my father's permission to ask for my hand. I was now thirty years old, and he was thirty-six. My father gladly gave his blessing and we began to plan for a life together. I would eventually move into Philippe's much larger home and learn how to manage a household with servants. There would be children; that was viewed as a given, for a man in his position needed heirs. He promised me that I would still be able to "scandalize the countryside" by riding whenever I wanted to; horsemanship was in my blood and he understood that riding was just as spiritual to me as holy communion.

Before we could have the banns read, my father died. His heart gave out one day in the grape arbor. We could not marry while I was in mourning, a ridiculous custom that required women to sequester themselves from public view except when necessity dictated otherwise. For an entire year, women in mourning swathed themselves in black clothes and veiling and were "left alone with their grief."

Philippe accompanied me to the bank so that my father's will could be read. He left the house to me, along with an income that would be distributed to me by the bank until such time as my cousin Francois Delacroix could be found and brought to Baincthuin from the Camargue to make arrangements. If I married, my husband would control the property and my income. Under the law, I was not permitted to determine how much money would be doled out from that income; for now, the bank would allow 200 francs a month. I could not even hold the bank account in my name as long as a male relative was available to manage the funds for me. It was a generous allowance, and I was grateful to have it. I thanked the bank president and we returned to my home in Philippe's carriage.

"Claire, if there is anything I can do to help find your cousin, I will. When your year of mourning is over, we shall marry at once. In the mean time, I need to make sure that you are well-cared for."

I pushed the veiling of my ridiculous mourning bonnet away from my face.

"I have never even met this Francois, Philippe. I think it silly that I cannot be trusted to manage my own money and that some stranger has a right to make those decisions for me under the law. How can this be right?"

"Claire, my dear, women just are not thought smart enough to manage their own affairs without a man to help them." His smile was rueful. "Of course, I think that those who made the laws would change their minds if they were to meet you. In the mean while, we haven't any choice."

He was right, of course, whether I liked it or not.

It took a couple of months to find Francois and bring him to Baincthuin. When he arrived, he came with several other Camargois horsemen with whom he had established a riding troupe. I enjoyed meeting his companions, but found my cousin to be somewhat cold and given to putting on airs. He even had a valet, which was peculiar for a man of his station. Francois moved into the Baincthuin house with me and his companions took lodging in town. Their horses joined Josephine in the barn.

I scandalized Francois and many others by putting off mourning a mere six months after my father's death. I wanted to ride, and so I did. I also wanted to marry Philippe and cease the pointless waiting.

No amount of black clothing would bring my father back. He had lived a happy life and I did not want to remember him in misery. I rejoiced in his memories of the Camargue, with its wild horses and colorful houses. I dreamed of having a home in the south of France, with terra cotta plastered walls and blue shutters.

To the shock of Baincthuin society, Philippe agreed with my point of view. The banns were read, and Philippe and I would be married within the month. Francois and his friends would be able to go back to their lives, as Philippe would be managing the disposal of my house.

And then came the fire.

CHAPTER 3

Paris, France
March 1889

Pierrot was tacked up in a heavy bridle, his eyes rolling with anger. I reached up to rub between his ears, causing him to relax and drop his head. I removed the bridle and knew at once that Francois had not seen to his tacking; he would never have put a gag bit on Pierrot. I was furious but gave no indication, instead making more soothing noises to calm the stallion. Once I judged that he was ready, I led him to a mounting block from which I vaulted onto the saddle.

At once, Pierrot reared and screamed in anger. I had no reins now and no stirrups, only the strength of my legs to stay on and the quickness of my wits to throw my arms around his neck, trying to weigh his forequarters down by sheer force. The stallion continued his wild dance, and yet no one came in response to my cries. Where in the name of Hades were the stable hands?

To my amazement, a tall figure appeared beside the angry horse. He wore evening dress, black leather gloves -- and a white porcelain mask over one side of his face. His hair was black as a raven's wing and he exuded confidence and mastery. He raised one gloved hand to the angry horse's neck, fearless of the waving hooves not far from his head.

I, on the other hand, clung to Pierrot's mane for grim death, willing the horse to cease his frightened antics. I looked into the stranger's green-gold eyes and, in that motion, shifted my weight just enough on the seat bones to unsettle Pierrot's balance. He returned his forelegs to the ground, stamping and snorting impatiently.

My rescuer wrapped his gloved hands around my waist and lifted me tidily from the horse; I noted that he smelled of sandalwood. He lifted the saddle flaps, undid the girth, and started in anger.

There was a short nail driven through the saddle flap, one that would not have affected Pierrot until I used my legs to grip but that would then have put him in agony. Horses' skin was so sensitive that they could feel a fly land; this was unconscionable. Whoever had done this had also, I was sure, put the gag bit on the horse, knowing I would remove it.

"I will see that this mischief is punished," my rescuer said, his eyes flashing. With a swirl of his cloak, he was gone.

I removed Pierrot's saddle, inspecting his hide. There were numerous punctures, oozing blood. I could not ride him in this condition; it would be inhumane. I fumed as I put a head collar on the suffering horse and returned him to his stall. Whilst filling a pail with water to bathe the poor creature's wounds, I found Francois.

"Find a runner; I cannot ride tonight. Look what has happened." I showed him Pierrot's hide and related my tale. "The saddle can be fixed. The horse's trust may even be regained eventually. However, someone wanted me hurt. Badly."

Francois grimaced. "Giraud said that you had given orders to be left alone with Pierrot, so we all went about other business. You do that at times; none of us thought the better of it."

It was true that I sometimes wished to be alone with my mount -- and my memories. Tonight, though, I had given no such order, and told Francois as much. Francois said he would look for a runner and I returned the way I came, prepared to return to my room and a book.

To my astonishment, Cesare stood in the paddock, a single rose braided into his tail with black ribbon. A note, on the familiar stationery, was tucked into his saddle flap; I opened the envelope and read the familiar hand: "Mademoiselle, it would honor me if you were to use my mount. I assure you he has been well taught. I will watch from Box Five. O.G."

As Francois approached, I decided nothing would be lost by trying. As I had with Pierrot, I mounted from the block and found Cesare responsive to my aids. The gentlest leg movement produced beautiful *tempis*. He collected himself at the slightest resistance on the bit and performed a *piaffe* that made my heart pound with excitement. I could ride tonight after all.

"Francois," I called, "Lead me to the wings. We are ready."

His shock at seeing me mounted on an unknown horse was surpassed only by his surprise at seeing the horse's excellent *haute ecole* schooling, and so he did as I asked.

It was not until I was in the wings, awaiting my cue amidst whispers of "Isn't that Cesare, the horse that disappeared last year when *he* stole it," that something else occurred to me. The horse's tail decoration was identical to the rose I had found in my room.

There was no opportunity to consider further, though, as it was now my time to take the stage.

As promised in the note, Cesare performed beautifully. I did not ask him to rear on command, nor to bow; those were tricks that I had taught Josephine over time. However, the remainder of the balletic freestyle *dressage* went well enough.

I returned to the paddock to cool the horse after his performance, wondering whether I should take him to the stall in the fifth cellar where I ordinarily found him. I decided to do so, but first I needed to change into more practical attire. I cross-tied the big horse and ran up the brief flight of stairs to my room.

Inside, I stripped hurriedly from the green gown and donned the breeches and loose shirt that I kept at hand. My green-topped boots completed the ensemble. I turned to the pier glass to brush and braid my hair before returning to the stable. For a brief moment, I could have sworn I saw my rescuer looking back at me, the strange half-mask balancing a face of such incredible masculine beauty that Lucifer himself might have swooned with envy. When I blinked, the illusion had disappeared.

"I must have been more frightened by the incident with Pierrot than I thought, if I'm hallucinating," I said to my reflection. I turned on my heel and went down to care for the horse.

I led Cesare down to the fifth cellar stall, talking to him the entire way.

"Nights like tonight," I said as I removed the horse's saddle and began to brush his coat, "I wish that Philippe were still alive. He would have loved to see you."

So it was that I spoke of something I seldom talked about: my fiancé, and the reason that my heart was so hardened to any advances.

"You see, Cesare," I finished as I braided his mane, "Philippe risked his life to go into the burning barn after Josephine, my mare. He himself was badly injured; the burns were horrible. I didn't care, and would have tended to him for the rest of my days. I still saw the man I had loved. I believe that all things are beautiful, if one only has eyes to see. Philippe died, not from the burns, but from an overdose of laudanum. There'll never be another for me."

I turned to work on Cesare's tail and was surprised to see my masked rescuer standing there.

"A tragic tale, Mademoiselle," he said, his tone cynical. "Is it true?"

"Why on earth would I lie to a horse, Monsieur?" My voice was a bit more sarcastic than I intended. "I loved Philippe." An unexpected tear coursed down my cheek and I wiped it away with the back of my hand. "No amount of ravaging to his face and form would have changed that."

I unfastened the ribbon that held the rose in Cesare's tail.

"I thank you for your assistance earlier, Monsieur. I do not know how you found your way here, or why. However, I am paid handsomely to care for this horse and I must do so now."

"I know, Claire," he said, stepping closer and looking down at me, causing me to realize again the disparity in our heights. "Cesare is mine."

My eyes widened in surprise. The stranger's beautiful mouth twisted into a cruel sneer.

"Do I frighten you?" He seemed to revel in the idea, and the thought irritated me.

"No, Monsieur, you do not." I spoke the simple truth.

I thought about what little I knew of this man as I finished braiding Cesare's "mud tail." Christine Daae, now the Comtesse de Chagny, had unmasked him on stage, revealing a face reputed to be so scarred and hideous that women fainted in fear. If he hoped to provoke that response in me, he would be sorely disappointed. Nothing could frighten me after Philippe's burns.

I turned again to face him.

"I am finished, Monsieur. May I return to my quarters?"

"Of course, Claire." His smile was a vicious slash in the beauty of his left side. "And please, call me Erik. It seems only right that we should use our given names with one another."

I made to sketch a curtsey and realized how foolish it looked in the breeches I wore. He seemed amused by the aborted gesture, but he took Cesare's lead and walked away from me.

"Erik," I called after him. "Thank you. For your help with Pierrot, and for the loan of your horse."

He turned back to me over his shoulder. "The pleasure, Claire, was mine. It's been nearly a year since I so enjoyed watching a performance from my box."

With that, he was gone.

I made my way back to my small room, grateful that the building was so quiet. It wasn't until I had changed into a night rail and settled into bed that I shook with the contained nerves of the evening. I could have been killed if Pierrot had thrown me.

I tossed and turned, sleeping fitfully and waking often from bad dreams. I heard a quiet voice, singing songs of love in such a beautiful, pure tenor that it wrung a tear from me. I was sure that whichever chorus boy was practicing at that hour was doing so to impress a soubrette in his chamber. Nonetheless, I fell asleep at last with the beautiful voice teasing my dreams.

CHAPTER 4

I woke the next morning to find another ribbon-wrapped rose on the night stand next to my bed. I inhaled its fragrance and wondered whether the Opera Ghost might have stood in my chamber and sung to me. The idea gave me an unexpected frisson of pleasure, particularly as I remembered the enchanting green-gold eyes that gazed upon me in the fifth cellar. Surely not. I was not given to such flights of fancy; I shook my head to clear the night's cobwebs away.

I laid out a gown to wear for the day; I would be shopping and could hardly walk around Paris in a divided riding skirt or breeches. The green wool was simple, yet elegantly cut, and I felt beautiful in it. I had a few pieces of jewelry to go with the dress, including a silver ring in the shape of a gargoyle with a faceted peridot in its mouth. I was fond of the piece, admiring the artistry and eccentricity of the jeweler who had designed it. But first, a bath.

I rang for the water boys, who soon appeared with a sloshing, steaming tub. I poured a bit of my rose-scented oil into the water and undressed. I luxuriated in the tub before finding my soap and scrubbing my skin. I then washed my hair and rinsed it in the cooling water. I stood in the tub and reached for a towel ... and watched as my mirror slid away into a siding.

Erik stepped into my room, attired in snug-fitting fawn breeches that showed off his muscular legs to perfection, a tailored shirt, and riding boots. Instead of the white porcelain mask I had twice seen, he wore a black leather domino. He carried a black shadbelly coat and a hat; a cravat was draped over his arm. These latter items he deposited on the bed next to my own garments.

"I wonder, Claire, whether you would accompany me for a ride today."

I wrapped the towel around myself and drew myself up to my entire diminutive height.

"How dare you! You enter my room at a whim! You demand my time! Agh!" I sputtered.

I did want company, if the truth were to be told; solitude and loneliness were friends whose fellowship grew tiresome. I sighed with more resignation than I felt.

"I have errands in Paris to do today. I will need to accomplish them before anything else."

Erik laughed insolently as the mirror slid back into place. I wondered what stratagem he employed to make it so. He picked up my regular corset, a pale blue China silk, and examined it somewhat disdainfully. My stays had no lace or fripperies; the only ornamentation was the fabric itself.

"Well, then, Mademoiselle, I suggest you don your chemise and allow me to lace you in. We can use my carriage." On seeing my expression he laughed, a trifle cruelly. "Oh, yes, my dear. I have a carriage. Money can buy a great many things. My face cannot be seen, lest I be recognized, but I do go abroad in the daylight. Now, don't dawdle, Claire."

I was too surprised to argue, so I slipped into my chemise and allowed him to lace me in. He dropped the petticoat over my head and tied its laces at my waist, and then just as expertly assisted me with the skirt and bodice. I drew the line at assistance with my stockings and boots, but he watched me don both with the same insolent expression on his face.

I brushed and braided my hair, twisting it up tightly and pinning it in place. I opened my armoire to reveal my small selection of hats and debated among two, a fancy one and a more serviceable poke bonnet.

Erik came up behind me and again I noticed the slight scent of sandalwood that surrounded him like an aura.

"The small green one with the black feathers, of course," he said, taking it down from the shelf which he could more easily reach.

I donned the hat, ring, and matching ear bobs with peridot drops. No precious gems for me anymore; semiprecious stones were all I could afford and I had but few of those. I opened a drawer and took out a pair of gloves. I slipped them on, buttoning the wrists.

Something inspired me to be slightly sarcastic when I was finished.

"Do I meet with your approval, Monsieur?"

He turned from the mirror where he had been arranging his cravat in perfect folds. He looked me up and down as he slipped his broad shoulders into the shadbelly coat that accented his flat abdomen and narrow waist.

"Oh yes, Claire. You'll do."

From the tail pocket of his coat, he took a list. "I need these items. You will pick them up as we conduct your other errands, of course, since I cannot be seen. I will provide the funds."

He opened the door to my room and looked out to make sure no one was in the area. We hurried down the stairs to the courtyard, where waited a closed coach with a driver. Erik stepped inside, and I gave the driver my instructions for the route to make my purchases.

As the carriage rolled out of the courtyard, Erik spoke again.

"So, your lover was badly burned, was he? Tell me how it happened. You see, I missed the majority of the tender tale you told my horse."

"We were to marry, Philippe and I. He was a very handsome man, and understood my love for animals. I've always had a gift for healing them." I looked just beyond Erik as though seeing into the past. "We were very happy, and I looked forward to being his wife. Philippe had a larger house, where we would move after our marriage."

A tear coursed down my cheek as I remembered. To my surprise, Erik's gloved finger wiped it gently away, his reach across the carriage sudden and tender.

"Go on," he urged; there was nothing of his previous arrogance in his tone.

"One day, there was a fire in the barn. I still don't know how it started. Philippe was visiting and we were having tea. I heard the alarm bell sound and started up quickly. I saw the smoke, and ran outside toward the barn, but Philippe was taller and faster. 'Stay back, Claire,' he said. 'Stay back.' I didn't listen, of course, but kept running even though he passed me by."

I choked back a sob.

"While I was seeing to the grooms and making sure that everyone was out safely, I heard a frantic neigh and realized that no one had seen to Josephine. Philippe ran into the burning barn, tearing off his coat. I tried to follow him, but the groom held me back. A few minutes later, Philippe came back out, his coat tied around Josephine's head, covering her eyes so that she couldn't see the flames. And oh, my god, the flames. Philippe's shirt and hair were on fire ... and ..."

I could no longer stop the tears, and so I cried quietly for a few moments. Finally I gulped a bit and went on.

"I looked after him in my home. The pain of his burns was incredible, and the physician left laudanum to help him. One day, I found him standing in front of a mirror, confronting his appearance. He turned and screamed at me to get out of the room -- that there was no possible way I was with him from anything but pity. That I could not possibly love such a monster as himself. That surely I would never want to make love with him again."

Erik sighed, his mouth twisting into a cynical grimace. "How well I know that feeling."

"But, you see," I rejoined, "that wasn't true. I loved Philippe with all of my heart and being. I still planned to marry him as soon as the doctor said he was well enough. I didn't care about his face. I cared about his soul."

"And did you ever tell him that, Claire?" Erik shifted to sit next to me on the leather seat of the carriage.

I nodded. "But he didn't believe me. Otherwise, he wouldn't have sent me off to care for Josephine, as I did every day while he napped. While I was out for those precious stolen hours, Philippe drank the rest of the laudanum. When I came back, he was dead."

I looked down at my gloved hands, twisting in my lap. "I kissed him before they took him away, Erik. That was the last touch of a man's lips that I felt, still warm because he hadn't been gone for long. After that, my cousin Francois sold the house in Baincthuin. He sold my jewels and my books. He sold everything but Josephine and my clothes. He made me come with him and his riding troupe, because my father had appointed him as my guardian unless and until I married. He still controls the income from the allowance my father left me; I see none of it."

I looked up at him. "That is all."

"Claire, I have known only one woman's kiss, and that one was quite ... reluctant. If what I ask of you now is refused, I will understand. Please, Claire. I want you to feel a man's kiss again."

With that, he lowered his mouth to mine. His lips were warm and gentle, but I could not imagine why I was surprised. Had I expected such beautiful lips to feel hard and cruel? I could not say. I slipped one gloved hand behind his neck, caressing the occiput of his skull, and returned the kiss with an ardor that surprised me. At last I broke away.

"How long, Claire? How long has it been since he died?" His voice was raspy with desire.

"A little over a year," I replied.

"Then perhaps," Erik whispered, his breath warm against my ear, "It is time to shed your veil of mourning and kiss me again."

As I turned my face up toward him, his gloved hand caressing my jaw, the carriage rumbled to a halt and the driver called out. "Mademoiselle, we've arrived at the modiste's."

CHAPTER 5

Cursing his timing, I called out my thanks and alighted from the carriage to make my first purchase -- but not without first drawing my own hand along Erik's freshly shaven jaw. I was no timorous virgin, and his kiss had enflamed me. I felt none of my usual caution or reluctance, only maddening desire.

Inside the modiste's, I could barely keep my mind on my task. Fortunately, I had a list inside my reticule. New stockings, that's right. Some beautiful lacy ones, instead of the practical worsted I had planned? I imagined Erik's gloved hands rolling them down after removing my round garters and shuddered a bit. His kiss had affected me more than I'd imagined possible. I gathered my wits about me and selected one pair of each.

I looked longingly at a window display: a beautiful evening gown in sapphire moire bengaline with a deep bertha neckline. I lifted its hem and examined the stitching, wishing I had use for such a piece. Not only was the price out of my reach, but I had no opportunity for dining out or attending the theatre. I sighed wistfully and returned to the carriage with my small package of ribbon, stockings, and so on.

"I saw you admire the gown in the window," Erik's voice came from the darkened carriage; he had drawn the curtains lest he be seen. When I closed the door after entering, there was no light at all.

"It is beautiful," I admitted. "But I've no need for a dress of that nature; I haven't the opportunities to wear such a gown."

"You like beautiful things," he whispered.

"Of course," I responded in surprise. "Most people do."

"Then how can you bear to look on me," he responded, still whispering. As the carriage moved away, he opened the drape to let the light in and reveal his unmasked face to me.

The left side of his face, his entire mouth, and jaw ... all were so handsome that they would take the breath away from an angel. The right side, though, was discolored and twisted. A port wine birthmark discolored skin so thin and fragile that lumps of misshapen bone and delicate blue veins could be seen through it. His left eye was fringed with thick black lashes; the right was barely lidded and sunken in the socket, but was the same soul-filled green-gold as its twin. The right side of his nose was also damaged, the soft nare non-existent.

"Look on this monster, and tell me again how you care more for the soul than the face," he said in a ragged voice.

"One moment," I said. I rapped on the roof of the carriage to get the driver's attention. "Instead of going on the green-grocer's just now, could we take a drive around the Tower site? I have so few opportunities to go for a drive. I should like to take my time."

The driver called his assent, and I looked back at Erik. I did not drop my eyes, nor did I cower in fright.

"Well?" His mouth was twisted in that cynical smile again.

"Erik, I don't know where to start. I know about Madame de Chagny ..."

The moment I mentioned the Comtesse, I was sorry. Something in his face closed away from me, and yet I could not take the words back.

"She was beautiful ... is beautiful. And she was a child. I have seen so much more of life." I reached out to touch the damaged side of his face. "This does not frighten me, Erik. Not in the slightest."

He leaned his cheek into my gloved hand, and surprised me by pressing his lips to my wrist through the buttonhole of my glove. I emitted a small moan of pleasure at the gesture.

"You enjoyed that." He drew away from my touch and slipped his mask back into place. "I have never known a woman, but I have read many texts from the Middle East. Some of them tell of ways to pleasure a woman."

He moved to the other side of the carriage then, and the moment was gone. Unfortunately for me, the feeling of his mouth on my wrist was not.

"The Tower," he mused as he looked out the window. "Eiffel's monstrosity will be the ruination of this City. Mark my words, mademoiselle; when the twenty years for this permit is gone, the people of Paris will demand that this eyesore be razed to the ground."

We finished our errands, his to the green-grocer and the baker, and to the music shop for staff paper, and I to the saddlery for new reins and the cobbler to collect a pair of boots I'd had repaired. We spoke of small things, simple pleasantries, for the remainder of the outing.

When we returned to the Opera Garnier, I thanked Erik for his kindness in lending me his coach and his company. He bowed over my gloved hand with a grace that would have made nobility look crass, and pressed his lips to my knuckles.

He straightened then and said to me, more gently than I could have imagined possible, "Claire, the pleasure was mine. You have given me something I never dared to dream possible, and I mean to repay you for it."

I could not imagine what he meant by that. I curtseyed to him and went up the stairs to my room.

I unlocked my door and had just put my purchases down when I realized I was not alone.

CHAPTER 6

"Giraud," I snapped, "What are you doing here? How did you get in?"

The stable hand sneered at me. "Think you're so high and mighty. Won't give me the time of day, and I see you getting out of some dandy's carriage. You're no better than you should be, that's what." He was drunk.

"Giraud," I repeated, "How did you get in here?"

"Had a key made, didn't I?" His laughter was cruel. "I've heard a man's voice in here, Claire. I know you're no ice maiden. Just needed some warming up, didn't you? I'll make you come around."

He advanced toward me and I flung my reticule at him, hoping to buy some time or to make him realize the foolishness of what he was about to attempt. Unfortunately, being short has its disadvantages, and my room was not large. Giraud slammed his hands into my shoulders and pushed me into the wall. I cried out for help.

"No one will hear you, Claire. Just like no one heard you when Pierrot tried to kill you. I've sent them all away. Now there's no one to distract you. Not your fancy horse, and not your fancy man with the carriage."

He set his foul mouth to my neck and was hiking my skirt up when I heard the snick of the mirror sliding back. Giraud was intent on his actions and noticed nothing. My eyes widened as Erik entered the room, an odd-looking thin rope in his hands. He motioned me to be silent, pulled Giraud away from me quickly and slipped the garrote around the would-be rapist's neck.

"You'll leave her alone, or I'll know the reason why," he whispered, as he tightened the strand. Giraud's eyes stood out as he desperately tried to breathe. Erik frog-marched him over to the door and pushed him out, releasing the garrote and locking the door behind him. Giraud fell down the stairs, cursing. I had no doubt he would think the entire scene a drunken dream.

At least, that was what I hoped.

I attempted to right myself. The bodice of my best dress was torn, my bonnet knocked askew, and my skirt was in a state of deshabille.

"I will change the lock myself," he said, still examining the door. He then turned around to me. "Claire, did he hurt you?"

"No," I whispered. "I'll be fine. I think."

I sat down on the bed and unpinned my hat.

"My dress is ruined, though. And what is that ... that ... thing?"

I indicated the gut string that he wound up and slipped into the pocket of his coat.

"It's a Punjab lasso," he responded. "I've become rather expert with it over time. One day, I will tell you about my time as the shah's assassin in Persia, but not now. Our priority right now is your well-being."

So, the rumors that the Opera Ghost was a murderer were true. I found myself grateful for his skill at that moment, but it gave me pause to realize the true complexity of the man who stood over me.

"You will not ride tonight. I will send a note to your cousin, and to the fools who manage my theatre. You need a night to rest."

I could see there was no arguing with him, so I didn't even try. I just sat there fiddling with the torn bodice of my dress, willing the fabric to return to its previous state of wholeness.

Erik opened my armoire and pulled out my breeches, boots and loose shirt. "Put these on," he said in a tone that would brook no resistance. "I'll return for you."

With that, he stepped out of the room and the mirror slipped back into place.

CHAPTER 7

I changed my clothes as requested, shoving the ruined dress into the back of the armoire; I would ask my modiste to make it into a skirt.

After a while, Francois knocked at my door, calling to me.

"Claire, I have a note here that says you are indisposed. It's signed O.G., of all things. Is this a joke?"

"Francois, there are some things that I am not at liberty to explain. I am not able to ride tonight. Perhaps you should ask Giraud why."

I opened the door to my cousin, whose ire was apparent. "What do you mean?"

"This afternoon, when I returned from my errands, Giraud was in this room. He tried to force himself on me, Francois. I will not be riding tonight."

"But what of this O.G business?" Francois demanded. He did not seem particularly concerned about my well-being, which annoyed me.

"You are right, cousin. It's a joke." I smiled grimly. "Now, I would really like to be alone. Could you please see to the horses for me?"

"Of course, Claire. And I will see to Giraud as well. I'll sack him for his insolence."

"As you will, Francois. As you will."

I closed the door behind my cousin and locked it. I then sat on the bed and allowed my fear to show. I cried great, racking sobs. The only man with whom I had ever made love was Philippe, and he was gone. With him, I had thought, had gone that side of me. Erik had awakened something inside me today and Giraud tried to take that something by force.

I curled up into a small ball on my bed and let the tears and sobs soak my pillow. It was thus that Erik found me when he returned.

At first he sat down next to me, his weight causing the bed frame to creak. He stroked my hair and sang quietly to me in that beautiful voice I knew so well, hearing the nightly serenade I had believed belonged to one of the Opera chorus. He then laid down next to me, wrapping his body protectively over mine. His hands were ungloved, with long, slender fingers ending in manicured nails. He caressed my face and continued to croon in much the same manner as I did when comforting a frightened horse.

"Come with me," he whispered eventually. He stood up and offered me his hand. "I have seen your home; now you will see mine."

I followed him through the open mirror, which slid back into place behind us. We were in a corridor that disappeared into darkness, moving inexorably downward. Erik carried a small lamp in one hand; he held my hand with the other. I marveled anew at the silent grace in his every motion. He wore loose trousers and an open shirt with his white porcelain mask in place, hiding his disfigurement.

We arrived at a small boat slip and Erik helped me into a tiny skiff. Using a gondolier's pole, he pushed off from the little dock. I saw discarded props along the side of the underground lake, and marveled at the unusual trappings of Erik's daily life.

A portcullis raised in the distance, and the boat glided through. It dropped behind us and I realized that there was some kind of a timing mechanism involved; there were only so many minutes to get through before one might be trapped under the heavy metal grate.

We landed at another boat slip, and Erik handed me out of the little craft.

"Welcome," he said quietly, "to my palace of music."

I looked around in amazement. There was a dining table, set for two; a music area with a violin, a piano, a pipe organ, and sheets of music spread all over the top of every surface there. A beautifully appointed bed was off to one side, with coverlets made of velvet and silk.

"I wonder, Mademoiselle Claire, whether you would join me for dinner? Perhaps you would like to change first?"

I must have goggled at him, for his laughter was rich.

"Just here, if you please," he said, moving aside a curtain to reveal a dressing room. On my way past him, I noticed several sketches of a beautiful young woman whom I assumed was Madame de Chagny. He clearly still carried a torch for the girl, and for some reason that pained me. I pretended not to have marked the drawings at all.

Inside the dressing room were the beautiful sapphire gown from the modiste and a pair of matching slippers. An elegant corset, of black silk embroidered with roses, black lace stockings with red garters, and a sheer lawn chemise with only the tiniest straps were also laid out.

"For you, Claire," he said quietly.

I turned to smile up at him. "Erik, I wonder if you would mind assisting me."

His smile turned cynical for a brief moment. "Am I always to play lady's maid for you, Claire?"

I slipped my boots off and undid the breeches I wore. I stood, in nothing but my shirt, and unpinned my hair so that it fell to my shoulder blades.

"Erik, I suspect there is nothing maidenly about you."

I was surprised at my own hoydenish behavior -- but not enough to stop it.

His movement to kiss me was swift and his breathing harsh as he plundered my mouth. I wrapped my arms around his neck and he lifted me easily. I locked my legs around his waist, and then broke the kiss as he shifted his hands to hold me up.

"My dress, my dear; I'll make us late for dinner," I smiled.

"Curse the dress," he groaned. "I could take you right now."

"I know," I replied. I unlocked my ankles and slipped down to stand before him. "But, I don't want it to be like that with you," I whispered as I caressed his cheek.

He turned his back to me then, his breath ragged.

"Put on the new chemise and hold up the corset for me to lace, Claire."

I did as he asked and he laced me up expertly. I sat down on a stool to don the stockings and slippers, but Erik knelt before me.

"Please, allow me."

He rolled a stocking and slipped it over my left foot and heel. Before continuing to unroll it, he bent forward to trace the edge of my anklebone with his tongue and I shivered, my eyes closed to greater savor the pleasure of his touch. He rolled the stocking the rest of the way up my leg, fastening the red garter around my thigh and draping the lacy stocking top over it in a perfect fold.

On my right foot, his thumb traced a gentle caress at the instep, followed by a soft kiss ... and then the stocking was rolled up and gartered in the same fashion. Gently he slid the beautiful blue slippers on to my feet.

"Your gown, Mademoiselle," he said, slipping it over my head and lacing it up the back. The dress perfectly flattered my curves, framing my bosom in black lace, and showing a deep expanse of pale décolletage. I could hardly believe my eyes as I looked into the mirror.

Everything was beautiful, except for my tangled hair. I raised a hand to it self-consciously.

"Did you think, Mademoiselle, that I was finished?" Erik gently brushed my hair, easing the tangles loose, until the chestnut mass fell freely to my shoulder blades.

"Now," he whispered from behind me, "lift your hair away from your neck."

Around my neck he placed an exquisite necklace of deep blue stones, the center teardrop piece nestling perfectly between my breasts.

"I have one more thing for you," he said, and opened another jeweler's box. In it was a sapphire diadem that he settled expertly into my hair. I looked like a queen, and could hardly believe my reflection in the mirror. I looked at Erik's reflection behind me, and saw a single tear course down his beautiful, perfect left cheek. I turned to face him.

"They are gifts for you," he whispered.

"I don't know how I can repay you."

"You have already given me more than you know."

"That's the second time you've said that, Erik. I don't know what you mean."

He knelt before me, taking my hands in his to kiss them. "Claire, you have given me hope."

He stood again, and gestured toward the dining area.

"I hate to keep a lady waiting, but I must dress for supper."

CHAPTER 8

I seated myself at the table and waited for Erik to reappear. When he did, he was in flawless evening attire: a tailcoat of Bath superfine, a black cravat, waistcoat of sapphire blue that was similar to the tone of my gown, beautifully fitted trousers, highly polished shoes and white kid gloves. I could not help my intake of breath at the mysterious, handsome creature before me, his porcelain mask somehow seeming both normal and natural.

Our meal was a simple affair of bread, cheese, cold meats, wine and fruit. Erik had no means of preparing a hot meal in his subterranean palace. Yet, a slice of bread spread with delicious Brie was like the finest filet that night. Erik removed his gloves and tore off a small bite of bread, besmeared the tidbit with cheese and held it out to me. I made to take it, not certain what he was about, but he shook his head no.

"Open your mouth, Claire," he whispered, and fed the bit to me. Taking food from his hand was a sensual experience and I decided that nothing would do but to imitate it. I sliced an apple into bits and gently slipped the pieces into his mouth, shivering as he licked the juices from my fingers.

Dear God, how I suddenly wanted him in a way that I had wanted no man since Philippe. I struggled to keep from tearing at his waistcoat and cravat as we continued to feed one another, no words passing between us as we reveled in each other's touch and closeness.

When the fruit and cheese were gone, Erik brought finger bowls and towels so that we might clean our hands. While I did so, he went to the piano, where he sat down and played an air that was unfamiliar to me.

I joined him at the piano, leaning against the black wood.

"Is that your own composition?" I inquired.

He nodded and continued to play the beautiful piece. He did not speak again until he was through, and then he turned to face me.

"What is it called," I whispered.

"It has no title yet, but right now, I think of it as your song," he said, not looking me in the eye.

I felt my knees go weak. It was at that moment that I realized what was happening. In fewer than two days' time, I was completely infatuated with the Phantom of the Opera. This was so unlike the practical view that I held of myself that I was nonplussed.

Erik put his arms around my waist, pressing his cheek to my abdomen. I stroked his hair, and realized that part of it was a false piece so expertly created that it blended seamlessly with his raven locks. I slipped it away from his head, and also removed his mask. I stepped back and took his chin in my hand, looking with longing into the face that was both angel and demon at once.

"Erik," I smiled, "I want to kiss you again." With that, I bent my mouth to his. He put his arms around me, and began to explore my lips with a velvet tongue. I groaned with the heat of desire that coursed through me.

Erik broke the fervent kiss first.

"I think," he whispered, "that perhaps I should return you to your room."

"No, my dear," I replied," I think it would be far more convenient if we went to yours."

His eyes widened in surprise, and he made to reach for the mask and hairpiece.

"No, Erik. I would have you as you are."

Wordlessly, he rose from the piano stool and led the way to the beautifully carved bed. The headboard was decorated with nymphs and satyrs: the bed of a libertine. Erik untied his cravat as I removed the diadem from my hair. His jacket, waistcoat and boots followed as I stepped out of the slippers and turned my back for my gown and corset to be unlaced. He kissed my neck and shoulders repeatedly as he did so, turning me to face him at last. His shirt hung open to the waist, revealing a flat, muscular abdomen with a sprinkling of black chest hair that met at the sternum and traveled down into the waist of his trousers.

I stepped out of my chemise and stood before him, wearing nothing but the stunning collar of jewels. I slid my arms under his shirt, feeling the caress of soft linen on the backs of my hands as I slid it down his warm shoulders toward his waist. There, I felt something else and drew away in shock.

He turned his back to me, shrugging out of the shirt, and I saw the cruel scars of a whip marring his body. He looked over his left shoulder, his handsomeness in stark contrast to the cruel stripes.

"I've known the lash, Claire," was all he said.

"My poor darling," I whispered, the word out before I realized it.

He turned on his heel and grasped my shoulders, standing before me clad only in his pants.

"By God, Claire," he moaned. "Please don't call me by endearments unless you mean them. I can't bear another hurt like the one I had from *her*."

I knew, of course, to whom he referred, and for a moment a spark of jealousy raced through my body. I stepped forward to caress him, my hand trailing down his chest to his trouser waist.

"I am not she," was all I said as I undid his waist and his trousers fell around his ankles.

He stepped free of the garments and stood before me defiantly, almost daring me to change my mind as my gaze raked over him.

"Are you certain? You've seen all," he hissed, a brief glimpse of the cynic returning.

"Erik," I said, leaning against the bed frame, "I do not know what the custom is in the books that you have read, but it is considered impolite to keep a lady waiting." I slid between the velvet coverlets, leaning on one elbow so that I could watch every move of Erik's strong body with its catlike motions.

He slipped in next to me and took me in his arms, lowering his mouth to my throat and nibbling there as I moaned. Then he trailed his mouth to my breasts. My nipples grew firm and hard under his ministrations, and I stroked his face and hair whilst murmuring endearments.

He raised his head then, surprising me with his next remark. "I have read that there are ways to make a woman more ... receptive ... and I would like to try them." His eyes were dark with passion as his hands caressed me. "Would you have me do so?"

I could only nod and whisper "Oh god, yes."

When he set his mouth to my sex, I gasped mightily ... and he stopped.

"Have I hurt you?"

"No, my sweet. Pray, continue."

I twined my fingers in his raven locks, moaning with ecstasy as he loved me with his mouth ... and then feeling a release of almost painful intensity combined with pleasure that left me writhing in delight.

I slid away from him.

"Lie down, darling," I whispered, "and let me love you the same way."

His breathing was ragged with desire. "I do not know if I can control myself, Claire," he whispered. "I want so badly to be inside you."

"Patience," I murmured as my mouth traced the line my hand had earlier drawn and my tongue caressed his perfect manhood.

His cry of pleasure echoed on the stone walls around us.

"My god, Claire ... no. I cannot wait to possess you."

He moved away from my touch and was on top of me before I could blink, sliding in between my thighs like we had always been together ... like fate. I wrapped my arms around his neck and kissed him deeply as he plunged into me and we moved together. I felt the sweet pain begin to bloom inside me again and I tightened my inner muscles around him, feeling the velvet steel inside me ... filling me. Then, with throbbing ecstasy, we released at the same time.

He settled in beside me, breathing heavily. I could see only his flawless left side; I had already noticed that he took care to be at my right as often as possible.

"Thank you," he whispered. "Thank you for ending forty years of tormented longing."

I didn't know how to respond at first. Of course, I was now a woman of the theatre; bad enough that I had behaved scandalously in

Baincthuin, but now I was only one step socially above a prostitute. That Erik might see me that way pained me greatly, and I lashed out without thinking.

"Is that what I am to you, Erik? A convenient trollop? No better than one of the soubrettes? A woman to be bought with gifts?" I gathered the blankets around myself, suddenly feeling ridiculous to be in bed wearing nothing but a necklace. I reached behind my head to undo the jewels, and the blankets fell down.

I made a sound of annoyance and, as soon as I had the necklace undone, pulled up the blankets again, putting my back to him.

Erik's hand caressed my shoulder.

"Oh, god, Claire. I am such a fool. I didn't ... Oh, god."

He got out of bed, and I turned toward him as he put on his shirt and trousers.

"How could you think that of me, Claire? How could you?" He went over to the piano and got his hairpiece and mask, putting them on before returning.

He knelt beside the bed and spoke quietly to me. "You are like no one else I've known, Claire. You are different from *her*, of course ... older, wiser, and ... compassionate. Christine left me her engagement ring to remember her by. She gave me false hope. You, though, you're a healer. I've watched you with the horses and with the barn cats -- with any hurt thing that comes in your path. I wondered if I might dare to seek you out, and now I've found that you've healed a part of me that didn't know it was hurt."

I was shocked at his declaration.

"No one can heal my face, Claire," Erik continued. "It frightened my mother so much that she turned me out. No one can heal the scars of the gypsy's lash on my back. But you healed the part of me that had no hope after Christine left."

He took my hand and laid it on his cheek. "I wish, more than you know, that I could do such simple things for you as escort you on a walk through the park, or sit with you openly in my box at the Opera, or even go into the modiste or the green-grocer with you on errands. I wish I could give you all that you deserve ... in thanks for what you have given me already."

"Erik," I whispered, "After Philippe, I intended that there be no one ever again. And yet, here you are. I could ask nothing more of you. I am so sorry for what I said. Please forgive me."

He stood up then. "My dear, I must get you back to your room and change that lock."

I got out of bed and went into the dressing room to don my breeches, boots and shirt again. Erik dressed as well, and brought the beautiful evening ensemble to me, folded carefully with the shoes and jewel boxes on top of it all.

"Don't forget these," he smiled.

I held the parcel carefully whilst in the boat and followed gingerly behind him, not wanting to drop the beautiful pieces in the dank corridor.

CHAPTER 9

When we arrived at the mirror panel that led to my room, I was surprised to see Francois and Giraud inside. Erik gestured for silence, and we watched and listened.

"You promised me," Giraud was saying to Francois. "You said she'd be here alone, indisposed-like. You promised I'd have her."

"I know, Giraud. I don't know where she is. I told you. I've no use for Claire, and you can do with her as you please so far as I'm concerned! I have her money, and that's all I want."

I was surprised, to say the least. So much for the promised sacking!

Francois continued his scathing remarks. "She's always thought she was better than the rest of us, and not even Philippe's death changed that. Who knew that the fool would rush into a burning barn to save her precious mare? He must really have loved the overeducated chit to do such a foolish thing. I was sure that she'd go in there and die. I'm just fortunate that her father's will turned her holdings over to me to manage."

Erik's face twisted in a grimace of rage. I laid a hand on his arm and whispered "No. Do nothing."

Giraud flopped down on my bed, the angry mark around his neck plainly visible. "She's no better than she ought to be, that's what. Her fancy-man tried to kill me this afternoon. And suddenly she's indisposed. You know as well as I that she's with him somewhere."

Francois looked at Giraud thoughtfully, and replied, "Now, even you know better than that. She relishes those rides before an audience.

As long as she's with her precious horses, she doesn't care about anything else. Which reminds me, I would love to know where that white Lipizzan came from. By rights, she should have been in bed with a concussion after what you did to Pierrot -- or even dead. And yet, there she was on a horse unknown to me, but well-known, it appears, to half the Opera Garnier cast. I'll find out." Francois smacked his fist into the opposite palm. "Let's away, Giraud. We have work to do."

I watched in horror as my cousin and his compatriot left my room, locking it with their own key just as Giraud had said.

After they were gone, Erik and I entered my chamber via the mirrored door. He opened my chamber door to see whether we had been noticed: We were not. He removed the old lock set with a pen knife and installed another one that he'd hidden in the voluminous folds of his cloak. He gave me one of the keys, and secreted the other in the tail-pocket of his coat. I was momentarily speechless with anger and hurt.

"They hurt my horses, Erik ... and wanted me dead." My voice was deep with anger.

For his part, Erik paced the room, cloak swirling about his ankles. "They will pay dearly for this," he announced, depressing the mechanism for the mirrored door. "I will return to you tonight ... my love."

With that, he was gone, the endearment hanging in the air even as the secret door slid shut behind him.

CHAPTER 10

From the pages of Erik's journal:

As the mirror slid closed behind me that night, I savored the words on my tongue. "My love," I had called her. To my surprise and delight, my affection is requited. She is interested in me for myself. What bliss to know this feeling after so many years of aching loneliness.

My joy was tempered, though, with anger at her cousin and his associate. I was mentally preparing a note to them ...

Oh, god. The accursed notes.

I had taken such pains not to let anyone know that I still lived, sending missives only to Claire and my friends Madame Antoinette Giry and the daroga Zareh, a friend from my days in Persia. In my concern for the woman I loved, I had sent notes to Messieurs Richard and Dupin, and to Francois. I had revealed my hand as surely as though I had appeared again in my guise as Red Death.

Perhaps all was not lost. Claire had told Francois the note was a joke from her, had she not? Perhaps I could retrieve the note from the imbeciles who managed what I still thought of as my opera house.

I stole across the stable yard to a secret tunnel that would take me directly to the managers' office and espied them in confrontation with Francois. Both parties had open envelopes in their hands: black-deckled stationery that was all too familiar. I groaned inwardly as I drew closer to listen.

"Francois," Dupin was shouting, "This is entirely inappropriate, and the joke amuses me not one whit. If what you are saying is true, and this chit of a horsewoman wrote these notes ..."

"From her own tongue I had the truth," Francois said. "She called it a joke."

"Well, Monsieur," Dupin announced, "we are unamused. With all that has happened in the history of this opera as a result of the so-called Phantom, we cannot afford another scandal. Your entire troupe is sacked, immediately. You have two days to be gone."

He turned on his heel and left the stable, muttering about having to refund a house and mount the piece currently in rehearsal ahead of schedule to make up the funds.

I was about to hurry back to Claire when Francois called for Giraud and told him what had come to pass.

"Let the others know, and make sure they know it was Claire. Perhaps this little problem can be solved for us."

Giraud's laugh was brutal. "I can think of several men she's turned down who'd like to teach her a lesson."

"Fine. Meet me back here in one hour's time. We'll go to her room and show her what happens to those who cost us so dearly."

Giraud turned to leave, and then asked a question. "What about her precious Josephine? I suspect Claire'll be in no hurry to ride again when we're done with her."

"Leave the beast for the knacker. It'll be another good lesson for my loving cousin."

With that they parted company, unaware that they had been marked -- or that they had raised my ire.

I knew that I risked exposure, but I had two missions to accomplish. I unwound the Punjab lasso from my pocket as I followed

Giraud down the stable aisle. He stopped in front of Josephine's stall, the mare huffing with her broken wind. Her knees were scabbed and obviously pained her.

"You're for dog meat, you miserable beast," Giraud laughed mirthlessly as he reached for her head collar.

At that moment, I struck with my weapon of choice and did not let go until Giraud had breathed his last. I pocketed the garrote, took two handfuls of Josephine's black mane into my gloved hands and vaulted onto her broad back. I would take her to the same place I stabled Cesare, and then I would return for Claire.

I galloped headlong out of the stable, mentally apologizing as I heard Josephine gasp for air under the strain of exercise, and hearing cries in my wake announcing that someone was stealing one of the horses. I only hoped that they would forget the sight of a masked man in evening dress on a black Friesian mare when they found their dead compatriot.

CHAPTER 11

I listened in astonishment as Erik told me what had transpired in the stable. He helped me stuff my few belongings into a pair of valises he'd brought through the mirror door.

"There's no time to lose, Claire. You have to come with me."

"But Josephine ..."

I still hadn't taken it all in.

"Your horse is safe, Claire. I promise you. Now, come with me."

I followed him through the mirrored door and watched him disconnect a simple lever system that allowed the mirror to slide in and out of the siding.

"It will never work again unless I put it to rights," he explained. "It buys us some time."

I followed him, almost running to keep up with his swift strides, to the little boat slip.

"I've sent notes to Madame Giry and Zareh, my friends. I know they will help you in any way they can."

"But what about you, Erik?"

I stepped into the boat and sat down to face him as he poled away from the dock.

"You will just have to trust me for now," he grimaced. "If, that is, you can trust a murderer."

I considered his words in a silence broken only by the splash of water as we glided under the portcullis and arrived at Erik's underground home.

"I suppose," I finally stated, "that Francois will soon discover I am gone, and presume I have indeed absconded with my 'fancy man,' particularly with Josephine missing. She's the only thing I own besides my clothes."

Erik doffed his opera cloak and settled on a chaise. I joined him there.

"You put yourself at tremendous risk for me, Erik."

He leaned up on one elbow and was grave in his response: "Claire, I would die for you and consider it a life well-lived."

"Don't say that," I whispered. "I couldn't bear to lose you." A single tear traced its way down my cheek at the mere thought of being without him. I wondered at how he had so thoroughly captured a heart I had thought locked away for good -- and in so short a time. Perhaps I was more lonely than I had admitted even to myself.

Erik leaned forward and kissed away the solitary drop.

"Only death will take me from you," he whispered, his breath hot on my ear.

He dropped his head, caressing my throat with his lips. "You're mine," he whispered. "Now and always. You are my heart ... my treasure ... my love."

His mouth trailed back up to my ear as he whispered words of love against my skin. I felt a pleasurable warmth spread through my body at his delicate touch.

I untied his cravat, loosening the perfect folds at his throat, and then unbuttoned his waistcoat. His shirt fell open, leaving him in a state of beautiful deshabille.

"Oh yes," I whispered, looking into his green-gold eyes as I removed his mask, "I am indeed all yours." I caressed his ravaged cheek as I rose from the chaise and strolled toward the bed, looking over my shoulder whilst unbuttoning my blouse. "Let me pleasure you again tonight."

I sat down on the bed's edge to remove my boots. Erik joined me, a trail of elegant attire showing his progress from the chaise. He stood before me without shame: there was no denying the perfection of his body. I caressed his manhood gently, feeling his tumescence rise and delighting in the groan of pleasure he emitted as my hands explored him. A teasing dart of my tongue made him shiver.

"My god, Claire ..." He laid down atop the velvet blankets and lazily caressed himself while I finished undressing.

I draped myself next to him, and then slid one leg over his waist so that I straddled him. I leaned forward, my hair caressing his chest and cheeks as I kissed him. His long musician's hands stroked my back.

"Now, my fancy man," I purred into his right ear, "Let me show you how I ride a stallion."

He gasped as I sheathed his manhood, sliding slowly down its length until our bodies were completely connected. I sat erect, my hands tracing patterns on his flat-muscled belly while my hips rocked as gently as though I were riding through the park on a sunny day. Soon, Erik began to match my movements, rising as I did.

I leaned forward to kiss him as we continued our coupling. I had never felt such tender ecstasies as I did with this man, and I wanted to consume him. Our movements became more rapid. I entwined my fingers in his hair as I kissed him more deeply, feeling my pleasure begin to peak. Then, my body exploded in a flood of sensations that left me gasping.

Erik wrapped his arms around me and turned over so neatly that I was astonished to find him looking down at me instead of up. He moved my legs so that they draped over his shoulders, willing my body to take him even deeper.

"My treasure," he moaned again, and I could feel his pulsating within me increase. With a cry of release, he collapsed over me, holding the majority of his weight on his elbows whilst tracing kisses along my hairline and brows.

He moved next to me, then turned on his side. I slipped into the curve of his body, and he wrapped his arm around me. I felt warm, protected, and yes, loved. His breath was warm on my ear as he whispered more endearments.

I realized, as the first warm drop struck my bare skin, that he was in tears. I turned to face him, and saw his beautiful mouth smiling so tenderly that it made my heart pound.

"I never knew," he whispered, "that I could feel this way. And yet I must send you away."

I started to protest, but he laid a finger across my lips.

"No, my beauty, not for good. Zareh and Madame Giry are finding a safe place for you. You must trust them. Zareh has our horses already. Once they have found a place for you ... for us ... we will be together."

"But, Erik ..."

"We have, at most, one day here together, Claire. I don't want to waste it in hearing useless protests. If only you knew how it pains me to love you this much and then ask you to go."

He buried his face in my shoulder and let the tears flow freely.

"Then, my dear," I said, my voice trembling, "Let us spend that day together, not in sadness, but in joy."

He nodded, but did not move away from me. So it was, for a time, that we clung to one another in silence broken only by an occasional sob and our breathing.

CHAPTER 12

After a time, I disentwined myself from him and sat up.

"My darling," I began, but Erik interrupted my train of thought.

"How wonderful to be called your darling," he smiled. "I could listen to you say those words for an eternity." Something lit in his eyes as he continued. "Do go on."

"I would love to bathe now. I presume that you have means available?"

His elegant left brow quirked and he laughed. "My dear, not only do I have means available, I have such means as will take your breath away."

I chuckled throatily. "I have no doubt of that; you've taken my breath away admirably so far."

He laughed aloud at my sally.

"Hoydenish thing, aren't you? And I adore it. My dear, I have a means of bathing that will permit us to do so together. I am delighted to show it to you." He got out of bed and extended his hand to me. "Come."

He led me behind the dressing room to a deep depression carved in the stone floor.

"I presume you've read of the Roman *caldariums*. This bath is based on the design," he said, moving a few brass knobs. Steaming water issued into the deep basin, to which he added a dollop of oil from a brass amphora.

"Sandalwood," he explained, as the scented steam rose to greet my delighted nose.

Erik turned off the taps after the tub had filled and then, picking me up as easily as though I were a child, walked down into the steaming water with me in his arms.

"Does this meet with your approval?" he whispered.

My response was to slip from his grasp and sink into the water so that only my head showed, my hair floating on the water around my shoulders.

"It's amazing," I sighed.

Erik smiled at my childlike delight in the warm, scented water. He made his way over to one side, where an alcove held mirror, soap and straight razor. He lathered chin and cheeks and shaved away the day's growth of whiskers. I slipped underwater and came up next to him, wet hair clinging to my back, and reached up to stroke his warm, smooth cheek. Once again, he pressed his sensuous mouth to my wrist and I moaned in pleasure.

"God, Erik," I breathed, "I would love to have you again."

"My dear, you will break me." His voice was warm with laughter.

He wrapped his arms around me then and massaged the sandalwood-scented soap into my wet hair, kissing my forehead gently as he did so.

"Lady's maid again," I smiled.

He leaned forward and whispered in my ear, "I would do anything for you. Now, lean back."

He supported my back and rinsed the soap from my hair in the steaming tub. The scent of sandalwood ... his scent ... surrounded me.

"Perhaps," I suggested, "You are in need of a valet?" I collected the soap from its niche.

In response, Erik dipped under water and came back up at a kneel so that our heights were better matched. I rubbed the soap into a lather and laved his thick raven locks. Bathing together was a new experience for me, and I reveled in the sensuality of it.

We stayed in the tub, talking; he about how Zareh and Madame Giry had saved his life at different times, and I about growing up an only child whose friends were books and animals. We bathed one another until the water became too cool for comfort. My fingers developed the little wrinkles that told me I'd been too long in the bath, but I wanted to be near Erik.

At last, Erik stepped out of the tub and collected thick Turkish towels from the dressing room. He brought them to the tub's edge before helping me out, and then rubbed me briskly until I was dry. A fine silver comb served to untangle my damp hair as I watched Erik replace hairpiece and mask. The contrast with his shameless nudity was marvelous.

"We must dress, my love," he said. "Madame Giry and Zareh will be here at any time, I am sure, and you must be ready."

"What of you?" I asked.

"I will follow as soon as I am able. I have a few things here I must see to before I can join you freely."

I rummaged through my valise, finding a serviceable black serge skirt and blue blouse. The plain worsted stockings I had just purchased came out next, along with my everyday corset and chemise, and a pair of walking shoes.

Erik dressed in loose black trousers and an open shirt while I donned chemise and corset, hooking it in the front rather than having him lace me in the back. Stockings and shoes next; I knew I was dragging my feet. Finally, the blouse and then the skirt over my head.

For his part, Erik was at the piano, playing a chord here and there and writing on staff paper. He must have felt my longing gaze in his direction, because he looked up at me and smiled.

"Claire, my muse returned this afternoon. I will be able to write again, for the first time since 'Don Juan Triumphant.' This means the world to me."

At that moment, a dark-skinned man in an Astrakhan hat came down a side stair that I had not noticed.

"Ah, Zareh," Erik said, standing. "May I present Mademoiselle Claire Delacroix. I presume you have been successful in your quest?"

"Yes, Erik, I have," said the Persian, of whom I now knew something from Erik's conversation. "Madame Giry is waiting in the coach for me on the Rue Scribe. Where are Mademoiselle Claire's bags?"

Erik handed him my two valises.

"I will take them to the carriage and then come back for Mademoiselle. Less than five minutes, Erik."

That was when I realized that Zareh meant for Erik and me to say our goodbyes.

I picked up my reticule and made my reluctant way over to the piano. Erik wiped the ink stains from his fingers and stood from the stool.

"I don't want to leave you," I whispered, unable to look at him lest I burst into tears.

"Claire, I promise you," he replied, taking my chin in his fingers and tilting my face toward his, "I will be there. Soon." He kissed me tenderly and then stepped back as Zareh reentered the room.

"Come, Mademoiselle," Zareh, said, taking my elbow to guide me. "We must away."

I took one last look at Erik before turning to head up the stairs; he was already seated at the piano and not looking in my direction at all.

CHAPTER 13

From the pages of Erik's journal:

I couldn't even bear to look at her as she left, lest I cry out for her to remain. The idea of separation from her pained me more than I imagined possible.

With a sigh, I stood up and looked around at the home I had known for twenty-five years. What would I take with me? What would remain here, hidden forever from sight? I had to choose carefully what would go with me in my trunks when Zareh returned.

The books, as many as possible; that went without saying. The violin, since neither piano nor pipe organ could be moved. The score I was currently composing: such a beautiful piece, and I could hardly wait for her to hear it. My clothes, of course, and my toiletries. I gathered things at random and threw them on the bed so that when I was ready to pack they'd all be in place.

My drawings? The score to "Don Juan Triumphant"? Deep in a drawer, contained in a small box, a ring of aquamarine and diamonds? All of those things seemed to belong to another Erik, another lifetime. They would remain.

As I thought about that ring, I had another inspiration and hurried to the piano to ink a few more notes into the score. My muse had taken serious hold and the timing could not have been worse. Yet, I continued to write out the score, changing a chord here and there but feeling the music flow through my hands like my own life's blood.

After what seemed mere minutes, Zareh returned to help me pack my trunks.

"Where is she?" I asked. "She is safe?"

Zareh laughed drily. "My friend, I think you will be surprised that she is hidden in plain sight. Antoinette found her a townhouse in the Place des Vosges, where Sorelli, Lisette and Jammes are kept by their paramours. Antoinette is there now, helping her unpack her things and keeping her company until I return. No one will think it odd that a woman lives there alone, save for her porter," at which Zareh pointed at himself, "and is visited at odd hours by a cloaked gentleman. For your part, Erik, you will stay at my house."

Zareh held up one last item from the bed, a music box in the shape of a monkey playing the cymbals.

"You still have this," he marveled.

I nodded, not wanting to admit that the box reminded me of the only friend I'd had for so long: a stuffed circus monkey.

"Please, Zareh, I would like for you to give it to Claire."

He nodded, tucking the device under his arm and picking up one end of my first trunk.

"Let us away, my friend," he said, and we carried the first trunk up to Rue Scribe.

We came back down and picked up the second trunk, and I looked around for the last time at my home under the Opera Garnier.

CHAPTER 14

When Zareh returned, he assured me that Erik was safely away from the opera house, and presented me with the musical monkey. Madame Giry's eye's widened.

"It is one of his most precious possessions," she said.

Madame Giry told me about the toy monkey Erik had clasped in his hands when she helped him escape from the gypsies and how he eventually replaced the disintegrating doll with the novelty sitting on my mantelpiece by having Zareh send for one from Persia.

Madame Giry ... Antoinette, I must remember, for she had insisted that we would be friends, wound the little handle on the box, and it tinkled a beautiful tune that she hummed. Obviously she had heard the box played many times.

"You care for him very much, don't you?" she asked quietly.

"Antoinette, Erik is very dear to me. He seemed so happy today. He even said his muse was back upon him."

Antoinette smiled then. "Oh, Claire, what a splendid thing. I will tell you, though, that when he is in this mood he will write his music from morning until night, barely pausing to eat or sleep. You may not see as much of him as you might wish."

"But he promised me ..." I couldn't help pouting.

"Erik does not make promises lightly, dear."

She then looked up at my mantel clock.

"I must be away. I'm sure Jammes will take me with her in the barouche that her latest paramour has provided." She made a small moue. "I told you there was no better place to hide you than here. No one will notice when Erik comes to you. And he will."

With that, Antoinette said her goodbyes, and Zareh followed shortly, explaining that he must see Erik settled and then would return to serve as my "night porter."

I remembered Erik's admonition to trust his friends ... and so I would.

CHAPTER 15

I went to a corner cafe for a cup of chocolate and some bread, and then returned to my new home. The townhouse was furnished in a rather baroque manner, all white and gold paint and rococo design. The bed was a four-postered wonder with draperies all the way 'round, and I mentally painted Erik's frame lounging across the matelasse coverlet. I felt my face flush as I further imagined making love to him. How he had possessed my soul so quickly, I could not explain. And yet, that was the truth of it.

The events of the past few days eventually caught up with my psyche, and I decided that the bed in question was indeed calling to me. I undressed, changed into a fine lawn night rail, and braided my hair. I could just catch the comforting aroma of sandalwood from Erik's soap lingering on my skin. I lit a lamp on the bedside table and picked up a novel I'd been reading. Yet, my mind raced so that I could not concentrate upon the story.

When Zareh returned, he came upstairs and knocked on my door, having noticed the light underneath.

"Mademoiselle, I am here. I shall retire to the parlor so that I might admit any guests you'd wish to see."

I caught the hint of humor in the Persian's tone; he knew there was only one guest I'd want to see.

"Come in, Zareh," I said, pulling the blankets up around me.

He entered the room, averting his eyes from the bed.

"Zareh, I want to thank you for your kindness to us ... to him."

"Mademoiselle," the Persian replied, turning his jade-green gaze to meet mine full-on, "I have never seen my friend so happy. Even now he is composing, and a more wonderful work I've never heard."

"I'm so happy to hear that, Zareh," I smiled. "Antoinette tells me, though, that I must not expect to hear from him when he is in such a frame of mind."

"Mademoiselle Claire, I think wild dogs could not keep him from your side e'er long."

With that, he closed the door behind himself and I heard his steady tread going down the stairs.

I again picked up my book, *Les Miserables*, but found I was unable to focus on the trials of poor Jean Valjean. My thoughts returned constantly to Erik and how I wished that he were with me. The memory of his enflaming kiss brought a blush to my cheeks and a flush of warmth to my body.

I put the book on the night stand, turning the oil lamp to a low glow. It would not do to trip and fall in the strange new place while seeking the W.C., after all. I settled under the blankets, my arms around a pillow and wishing it was my lover near me. How could I miss him so, after such a very short time?

I awoke in a fully darkened room, and was disconcerted until I heard his beautiful voice, singing softly to me: a song of surrender in the darkness.

"My dearest," I whispered as I heard the sound of a lucifer striking. Erik lit a beeswax taper in an elegant silver holder, which he then placed on my night stand. The flame's glow gave a ruddy light to his raven hair.

He doffed his cloak with an elegant swirling motion and laid it across a chair. Gloves followed, and then cufflinks. He never took his eyes from me as he continued disrobing in silence, finally removing the leather domino mask.

He slid into bed next to me, still not speaking, and pressed his mouth to my breast, laving and teasing my nipple to hardness through the sheer fabric of my night rail. I moaned in pleasure at the sensation.

Erik ceased his ministrations only briefly, to undo the buttons at the throat of my garment, slide it over my head, and undo my braid so that my hair hung loose. His green-gold eyes were dark with desire.

"You have shown me how you ride a stallion," he whispered as he caressed me. "Now let me show you how I compose an opera."

His breath was warm on my ear "First, there is the prologue."

He trailed his mouth down my cheek and to my lips, where he took his time exploring my mouth with his tongue. I entwined my fingers in his hair and returned his kiss with matching ardor.

Each second that he took as he kissed down my neck to my breasts was torture and pleasure at the same time, his tongue teasing my skin. When he set his mouth to my mons, I was already tremulously close to climax. He brought me just to the very edge before plundering my mouth again with a tongue that tasted of my own fluids.

I caressed his hardened manhood and whispered to him, "I want to taste you."

His response was to lie back against the pillows, the candle's glow lending a golden aura to his beautiful form.

I kissed his throat, then down his sternum and flat abdomen, until at last my tongue was swirling around his tumescence. His hips moved gently as he caressed my hair.

I could feel the pulsating desire in him, and at last he moaned,

"Claire, I can't wait any longer."

I laid down next to him and turned on my back so that he could enter me. We were both trembling with desire, and the sounds we made during our coupling were more animal than human: purrs, growls and, at last, cries of ecstasy.

As we lay together, his arms around me, I chuckled.

"What is it?" he asked.

"So, this opera you were writing just now. Was that the *denouement* or the *entr'acte*?"

His hearty laughter filled the room. "Claire, I assure you, that was merely the prologue."

CHAPTER 16

From the pages of Erik's journal:

I left her with great reluctance that morning, before sunrise. Yet, we both knew it must be so.

I returned to Zareh's home on Rue Montorgueil in Les Halles. The best thing about living so near the marketplace is the ease with which I may purchase gifts for Claire. She has been deprived of so many things because of her cousin's greed. Fortunately, Zareh indulges me by purchasing the things I see in the windows by night.

The second day that I visited Claire, I brought beeswax tapers scented with sandalwood and attar of roses. The light is so much more pleasant than the oil lamp. I also brought a hamper of cheese and meats from the market stalls so that we could have a quiet, cold supper. While Claire's townhouse has a kitchen, it has been so long since I prepared a hot meal that it is easier this way.

Over the course of these past several weeks, I have brought her more clothing and jewels. I am sure that Claire's favorite modiste thinks that Zareh is her new patron, what with the number of outfits he has ordered to fit her. I think it embarrasses my modest Muslim friend as much as it amuses me.

My muse has been on me even stronger of late, and it delights me to know that I am still inspired to compose. Any time that I must spend away from Claire is, nevertheless, almost maddening.

The most difficult thing about our courtship is that we live a sort of nocturnal existence. There is a beautiful park in the Place des

Vosges where we sometimes walk by night, but it would be so much more pleasant to do so during the day. No matter how fine the wrap I bring for Claire, or how warm my cloak, we are still together only during the cold hours of darkness. The necessity that hides us from prying eyes also deprives us of a normal courtship, a situation that I find unfair to Claire.

So, we go for our nighttime walks, and we talk about something Claire read in the newspaper or the gossip that Antoinette Giry brought her way. Sometimes I bring my violin and play for her. Many nights, we sit in front of the fire, holding one another and saying very little at all.

It almost goes without saying that we make love. When the morning dawns, I curse the daylight because it takes me away from Claire's side.

Tonight, though, I will make up at least some of the inconvenience to her. I have sent the billets with Zareh to have her sit in Box Five at the Opera Garnier for the performance of "Aida," and I will meet her there. This much of a normal courtship I can give to her.

I dressed that evening with care, donning the sapphire blue gown and jewels Erik had given me. My hair was pinned in a loose chignon, crowned with the sapphire diadem. The billets for the night's gala performance were in my reticule. Zareh had a small coach waiting in front of the townhouse, with Josephine in harness. My mare was doing well under the ministrations of Zareh's hostler, and I was delighted to see her.

I examined my reflection in the cheval glass one last time before collecting my wrap, and then decided to reread Erik's brief note one last time.

"My dearest Claire: my apologies for my extended absence. I have finished my composition and will delight in seeing it performed for you one day soon. Kindly do me the honor of sharing my box at the Opera Garnier Saturday evening. I assure you, I will be there. E."

My gloved hands trembled a bit as I replaced the black-deckled card in its envelope. I had missed him more than I'd imagined possible. I tried to keep a normal life, going to cafes, galleries and museums; always, I imagined Erik there with me. Zareh and Antoinette visited me during the day and kept me company lest I become entirely a creature of the night. My life certainly had taken a peculiar turn.

Zareh tapped at my door.

"Mademoiselle Claire, it is time to go."

I collected my wrap and went downstairs, where Zareh handed me into the carriage and I was again alone with my thoughts for the short ride to the theatre. How I wished Erik were seated across from me, as he had been that day when he revealed his ravaged visage to me, and then kissed me for the first time. I felt a blush rise to my cheeks at the recollection.

The carriage rolled to a stop and a liveried footman assisted me in stepping down. I showed him my billets and he directed me to an usher. He, in turn, looked surprised at the seating but showed me to the box.

"Are you sure you want to sit here, Madame?" he inquired. "It is said 'round these parts that a ghost haunts that box."

I inclined my head. "I fear no ghost, Monsieur. The ticket is a gift from a friend."

The usher's eyes widened and he sketched a bow before going to assist another patron.

Antoinette Giry appeared at my elbow with a program, which she handed to me.

"He's inside the box, Claire. The column to your right when you go in is hollow; that is where he is. When the music begins, he will come to you. Then, he will return to the column during the *entr'acte*," she whispered, giving my arm a squeeze. "Between the two of us, my dear, I have never seen him so happy."

I thanked her and entered the box; Antoinette drew the velvet draperies behind me.

Once inside, I took the seat closest to the front; the other was slightly to the right and rear of me, and I knew that Erik could watch the opera from there without being seen. I, on the other hand, was fully visible and would give every appearance of being alone in the allegedly haunted box.

I tried to focus on the program and finally gave up. I opted instead to watch the steady flow of elegantly dressed opera patrons. I mentally blessed Erik for the gown he'd bought me. I fit in, and no one in the stalls or other boxes appeared to make the remotest connection between me and the horsewoman who had entertained them in the past.

At last, the bright stage lights flared on. I heard a rustle just behind me, and then a white kid glove settled briefly on my shoulder as Erik leaned forward.

"You look so beautiful, my darling," he whispered.

I leaned back so that my mouth was against his closely shaven cheek and pressed a kiss there. I turned to look at him: the flawlessly beautiful face that I could see, and the white porcelain mask covering the rest. He was again wearing elegant evening attire, and looked devastatingly handsome. My eyes spoke my longing.

"Watch the performance," he urged. "Time enough to look upon me."

He moved his chair a little closer to mine so that he could hold my hand -- but not so close that he could be seen. It was thus that we passed the first act.

During the last number before the *entr'acte*, Erik pressed his lips to my wrist through the buttonhole of my glove, a gesture that he now knew made me shiver with pleasure. Then he slipped into the hollow column, just as Antoinette had explained he would do.

Antoinette brought a glass of champagne to me during the *entr'acte* and sat with me for a while.

"Erik has asked me to tell you during the intermission that his latest composition will be performed soon in the village of Montfermeil-sur-Mer," she said. I must have looked very surprised, as she patted my hand in a comforting fashion. "Zareh and I will take you, my dear. You must not miss it. And now, I must return backstage to my corps de ballet. I will see you soon, my friend."

When the second act began and Erik was seated near me, I leaned back to question him in a whisper.

"What is this composition, and why is it being performed thirty miles away? And when is the concert?"

"It is a surprise for you," was all that he would say. "I am finalizing the arrangements."

Our evening out passed far too quickly for me. Before the final chorus ended, Erik once again absented himself. When the performance was over, I collected my wrap. The same usher opened the draperies for me.

"Did you see the ghost, Mademoiselle?" he asked me.

I smiled as I gave him a sou for a gratuity. "Monsieur, I assure you that the only things I saw tonight were entirely real and alive."

Zareh brought the coach around then, and a footman held the door for me as I stepped up. When the door was shut, Erik was there.

"I have been too long away from your side, Claire. And tonight, that is where I wish to sleep."

I settled into the crook of Erik's arm, my face against his cloaked shoulder.

"Thank you for sharing the opera with me tonight," I smiled.

"The pleasure, my dear, was mine."

We remained in companionable silence until Zareh drew the carriage to a stop before my *pied-à-terre*. Erik stepped out of the carriage first, assisted me in alighting, and then collected a valise from within.

"I think, good Daroga," he said to Zareh, "that Claire will be safe in my company tonight. Perhaps you could come tomorrow morning to collect me?"

Zareh smiled his assent and clucked to Josephine, who trotted off smartly.

CHAPTER 17

I unlocked the door of the townhouse and we went inside. Erik removed his cloak and gloves, then sat down on the divan.

"Join me," he said, patting the cushion. "Surely you would like to be free of those heavy jewels if nothing else."

"I don't know why I feel so nervous, all of a sudden," I said as I took the proffered seat.

"We've never actually spent a night together, have we?" he inquired as he unhooked my necklace. "Is that it?"

"I suppose so. Oh, Erik, I have so desperately wanted to wake up next to you."

"Is that so," he whispered, grazing my cheek with a kiss as he unpinned my hair.

I nodded.

"My dear, we are of one accord in that." His smile was almost sinful. "Let us be abed, then. I've not slept as much as I might have liked; I have such distracting dreams of you."

He collected his valise and followed me upstairs. Erik unlaced my dress and corset, and I donned a fresh night rail from my clothespress. Erik changed from his evening attire to a pair of loose-fitting black silk pants. As he turned away to close the valise into which he dropped his mask, I was again struck by the cruel scars on his back. How anyone could do such a thing to a living creature of *any* kind was beyond my ken.

I sat down at my vanity to braid my hair for the night, but Erik took the brush from my hand.

"Let me."

He gently brushed my hair out over my shoulders, as I watched in the mirror. His hands were deft as they plaited my locks together. Then he bent to kiss my throat.

"Tonight, my beauty, let us sleep entwined together," he whispered. "I want nothing more than to wake up next to you."

Erik turned back the coverlets of the bed and slipped between the sheets. I turned off the lamp and slid in next to him, and his body curled around mine protectively.

"I love you," I whispered, voicing my feelings for the first time.

Erik sighed in contentment.

"Sleep well, my treasure."

From the pages of Erik's journal:

The last words she said to me that night were "I love you." Were ever words more beautiful? After so many years of longing to be loved for myself, to have it happen has been a dream come true. She is like no one I have ever known. So proud, intelligent: so sure of herself.

When I awoke that Sunday, she was already up and about. She came into the bedroom wearing a silk morning wrapper in a shade of violet that lit her eyes perfectly. She carried a tray with a teapot and some brioches from the corner boulangerie.

"Your breakfast, darling," she said, and placed the tray on the night stand. She sat on the edge of the bed and caressed my shoulder. I sat up, pulling some of the pillows into place behind me as she poured a cup of tea.

The entire scene was so strange to me. Most couples enjoyed these simple pleasures, yet to me it was all very new. We shared the tea and brioches, and spoke of books. She is well-read and her observations quite astute. The time passed quickly, and I was very disappointed when Zareh arrived to spirit me back to his home.

Claire stood on her tiptoes to kiss me goodbye at the door and it was all I could do to refrain from shouting from the rooftops that I would stay forever.

That time will come soon enough.

CHAPTER 18

Erik and I enjoyed one another's company at the house on Place des Vosges whenever his composing permitted. For my part, I was having a little trouble adjusting to a lifestyle both more nocturnal and more leisurely. I was so accustomed to rehearsing, or looking after the horses, that I sometimes found myself at loose ends.

I began to venture out, cautiously at first but then more freely. Paris was so large and busy that I could go about my business without being marked by anyone I knew, so long as I stayed away from the Opera Quarter. Visiting the Louvre was my favorite pastime; I loved viewing the masterpieces of sculpture and painting that were kept there. I could take exercise by walking up and down the many galleries at the same time I was looking at the collections.

I also enjoyed visiting Les Halles, the market stalls. One never knew what one would find. Fruits and vegetables, meats and cheeses: the finest foods in season. There were booksellers, weavers, chandlers, soap-makers; the variety was astonishing. Even on days that I chose to buy nothing, walking around looking at the goods and watching the people was very entertaining for me.

The nights that Erik did not come to me, I slept deeply. I felt very serene and safe with Zareh as my concierge. Some evenings, he and I would enjoy a game of chess. Zareh always bested me, but my skills improved with each match.

Those nights with Erik, though, were more precious than rubies to me.

He told me of his life in Persia, where he lived among the Shah's harem because they thought him as safe as a eunuch. How naive both the Shah and his women had been! He also spoke freely of being paid to serve as the Shah's assassin, and of the various traps he had built into the palace in Tehran at the Shah's behest.

I was surprised to learn that he had replicated one of those traps, a mirrored room with a hangman's noose, in his home under the Opera Garnier. The idea of living near a torture chamber disturbed me mightily. Yet, there was so much about Erik's life that I did not yet know; I found that I could not judge him. I was fortunate to have known only love and kindness until my father's passing. Erik's life had been the very opposite of mine in that regard and I could not imagine what that might do to the psyche of a child.

We spent only the occasional full night together, waking in one another's arms. Those nights were the most precious of all.

A midnight cold supper in front of the fireplace was one thing, but waking to share breakfast was just plain wonderful. Sometimes I would slice saucisson and bread from the market stalls, and we would toast them over the coals. Other times, Erik would take over the kitchen to prepare eggs and brioches.

No matter, though; our time together always felt entirely too short. I longed to spend every day and night with him, and to hell with whatever scandal it might cause.

CHAPTER 19

June 1889

After a somewhat longer than usual absence, I had a note from Erik on a Wednesday evening in June, stating that Zareh and Antoinette would collect me at eleven o'clock on the following Saturday morning for the drive to Montfermeil-sur-Mer. His composition would be performed at two o'clock that afternoon. I was consumed with curiosity about Erik's work, and none of my wheedlings netted the slightest bit of information from either of Erik's apparent co-conspirators. All either of them would do was smile and tell me that I would know come Saturday.

On Friday afternoon, Antoinette stopped by with a package for me: yet another box from my favorite modiste.

"A gift from Erik," she explained, "which he hopes you will wear tomorrow for the performance."

Inside was an elegant ivory moire walking suit. I was glad that I had a duster coat to wear over it; I would not want such beautiful garments to be travel-stained.

"I will see you tomorrow, my friend," Antoinette smiled as she departed. "Sleep well."

There was a rare joke! It was far too long since I'd last seen Erik, and all I knew was that he was giving a mysterious concert in another town. I doubted I'd sleep a wink. Nevertheless, I would try. I wanted to look my best at this performance, knowing Erik would be there somewhere -- perhaps hidden, perhaps not -- and would want to see me looking well in the beautiful clothes he had sent for me.

When I did go to bed, I fell asleep quickly. In fact, when I awoke I was somewhat surprised at how deeply I had drowsed despite my curiosity and anticipation of Erik's concert. I arose, went about my toilette, and dressed myself. I despaired of creating an elegant coiffure, though, and again resorted to a loose chignon. Erik had given me an ivory straw riding hat with mauve flowers and ribbons; it coordinated beautifully with the walking suit and I decided that I made a satisfactory appearance.

When Zareh knocked at the door, I was ready with my duster coat and reticule.

"You look beautiful today, Mademoiselle," he said. "Madame Giry is already in the coach. We must away."

I locked the door behind myself and allowed Zareh to assist me into the carriage.

"Good morning, Antoinette," I smiled. "Are the two of you still going to keep me in the dark about the performance today?"

"My dear friend, I think it best that Erik tell you himself when we arrive. He has been looking forward to this ... performance ... for quite some time." She patted my hand. "Now, I will be about my needlework and perhaps you will find a way to while away the time?"

I had a small volume of poetry in my reticule, but I could not concentrate on my reading. I watched the scenery go by as we rode the thirty miles from Paris to the little seaside village, occasionally returning my attention to the book. My mind kept wandering to the very closed-mouthed behavior of my friends, and curiosity about the concert Erik had planned.

When at last Zareh stopped the coach and opened the door for Antoinette and me, I was rather surprised to find that we were in front of a church.

"Erik's composition is being performed here?" I asked.

"Yes, my dear, it is," Antoinette said as she alighted next to me. "Now, let us have your duster, shake out your skirts and go inside."

As we entered the sacristy, a beautiful piece of music was being played on the organ. I recognized the leitmotif as the one that Erik had played for me in his former home. The completed opus had a grandeur about it that took my breath away.

"We are late," I said to Antoinette. "They have already begun the performance. And I still don't know what it is."

Erik appeared at my elbow then, dressed in an elegant gray morning suit, unmasked but with his hairpiece in place.

"No, my love; you are exactly on time." He offered me his arm then, and walked me into the sanctuary.

Halfway in, he stopped, and I made to seat myself in one of the many empty pews.

"What is this piece, Erik? It is so beautiful."

"My dear," he whispered as he lowered himself to one knee, "it is a wedding mass that I have written. For us."

I was speechless. Things had happened so rapidly between Erik and me. He remained on one knee as the beautiful music played on.

"Claire, my love ... my treasure," he murmured. "Will you do me the honor of being my wife?"

I could not stop the single tear that coursed down my cheek. After Philippe, I had intended never to wed. Yet, Erik had reawakened me ... and I nodded my assent as I realized that the idea of life without him was abhorrent.

"My dear, I can't hear you," he teased.

"Yes, Erik. I will marry you."

He then took a small box from his pocket.

"I remembered an unusual ring that you wore once in my presence, and I sought out its maker. I hope that these will meet with your approval." He opened the box to show me two pieces. One was a simple gold band, clearly made to fit Erik's hand. For me, Erik had selected a gold band in an intricate floral motif that could only have been made with lost-wax casting. It was set with a large stone that flared green-gold like his eyes: a tsavorite garnet, and very rare indeed.

"Beautiful," I whispered and caressed his cheek.

"Well, then, let us not keep the good vicar waiting."

I stood then, and Erik led me to the front of the sanctuary. The vicar, Antoinette and Zareh awaited us there.

CHAPTER 20

From the pages of Erik's journal:

Oh, happiest of days: the day I never thought to see. I have married Claire; she is now Madame LeMaitre. My wife. Were happier words ever written?

The weight of a wedding ring on my finger is new to me and brings me great joy. To stand there, before a vicar and our two good friends, and exchange vows of fidelity with the woman who fills my soul. I find that words fail me.

She wanted to know why we had gone so far from Paris. The truth is simple. Zareh has a home in this little town, and knows the vicar. He was able to arrange the paperwork for us without going through the formalities of reading the banns. For a fee, of course.

As I write these lines, I am inside the carriage waiting for her. She is there, in the beautiful gown I had made for her, saying her farewells to Antoinette and Zareh. Her ring shines on her finger, and I am filled with pride. Tonight, in Zareh's country house, we will share our first night as husband and wife.

After the brief ceremony, I said goodbye to our friends and joined my husband in the carriage that would take us to Zareh's country home. He had kindly loaned it to Erik and me for our honeymoon. I could not stop smiling with delight, I felt so filled with love.

I sat next to Erik on the carriage's leather seat, nestled in the crook of his arm, and sighed with contentment.

"My love," he whispered, his lips grazing my forehead. "My wife."

I had a realization then and sat up straight.

"Darling, what on earth are we going to do about clothes? I came with nothing but this dress and my reticule."

His laugh was warm and throaty.

"My dear, there are advantages to knowing which modistes you favor, to say nothing of having friends who are willing to help me expend my funds. I think you will be pleased with the trousseau awaiting you."

"You did not have to buy new things for me, Erik," I said solemnly. "I have always looked to my own needs."

"Consider it a wedding gift then," he rejoined. "I wished to buy the garments for you, and I did so."

I sighed in resignation. "Very well. And what matrimonial gift would you have?"

Erik took my hand and grazed my knuckles with his soft, warm lips. "I have all of the gift I could possibly desire," he murmured as he looked into my eyes.

I could feel the blush rise to my cheeks, but I determined to find an appropriate present at the earliest convenience.

When we arrived at our honeymoon cottage, I was immediately charmed with the area. We were on the outskirts of the town, in a stone house surrounded by lavender and roses. It reminded me of my old home in Baincthuin; the scent of the garden was heavenly and the setting picturesque. I envisioned charming boulangeries, charcuteries and greengrocers; indeed, I looked forward very much to exploring the area.

Erik arranged for the driver to return in two weeks' time and then unlocked the door to the charming little house. I was about to go in, when he scooped me up into his arms.

"I believe there is a certain tradition to be observed here, Madame," he smiled as he carried me through the door. I laughed and kissed him full on the mouth, my fingers raking through his black locks.

"Mmmm. Time enough for that, my dear," he said as he sat me gently on a divan. I promptly stood up and began looking around the cottage. It was small: a sitting room with a fireplace, a kitchen and dining room, a water closet, and the bedroom. Next to the bed were boxes from my favorite milliners and modistes. On the bed was laid out an exquisite night gown and peignoir of pale green silk and creamy lace.

Erik came up behind me and wrapped his arms around my waist. "I can hardly wait to see you in that," he whispered in my ear. "Antoinette thought it would be perfect for your first night as my bride. Now, open the rest of your boxes."

As I opened the packages and examined the beautiful dresses, blouses, skirts, underpinnings and hats, I was amazed. Erik's taste was exquisite. The fabrics were of the highest quality, and all in the latest styles.

"Thank you," I smiled as I folded the garments and put them into the clothes press. "I don't think I've ever had such beautiful things."

"You'll want to change out of that pale suit, I should think," Erik responded as he doffed his suit jacket. "Perhaps something more practical for our walk into town?"

I was somewhat surprised, and said so. I had not expected him to leave the house.

"My dear wife, this is not Paris. I am not known here. Perhaps people will presume I've an injury. A burn or something of that sort. I will not hide any longer, Claire; I want to live again and I am starting now."

He removed his cravat, braces and shirt, and sat down on the bed to take off his shoes.

"I want to have the pleasure of going to the market with you," he continued. "All of the things I said before about wanting to walk in the garden, to be seen openly with you: I intend to do all of them." His delight in the idea was palpable.

I changed from the elegant, pale silk into a charcoal gray dress with black soutache trim. I was reluctant to cover my beautiful wedding ring with gloves, but propriety demanded it of me. A plain straw hat with a broad brim and gray ribbons would do for a walk into town.

Erik had changed to a simple shirt and trousers and donned a loose-fitting black jacket. A soft fedora in the same color shaded his face and its porcelain disguise.

"Madame LeMaitre, shall we go to market to select our wedding supper?" He extended his left hand to me. The gold band shone proudly on his finger.

"I would be delighted," I responded as I took it, and we walked out the door and down the lane into the village.

CHAPTER 21

The day was warm, with a pleasant mild breeze. We strolled in companionable silence into town, delighted to be in one another's company without the artifice and subterfuge we had employed in Paris. Just being abroad together in daylight was a grand treat.

As we entered the village proper, I noticed that there was some kind of circus in town; the tents were set up in the market square. Erik stiffened at the sight.

"Let us be about our business quickly," he muttered. "I've no desire to be in the vicinity of one of those traveling fairs ever again."

I nodded my assent, thinking of the whip scars that crisscrossed his back.

I opted to visit the greengrocer first. I selected a basket from those available for sale, and examined the *haricots verts* and *aubergines* with the grocer's assistance while Erik purchased a newspaper from a nearby stand. I purchased the beans, along with some salad greens, and then moved on to the butcher, where I selected two very fresh-looking filets. I planned to avoid the fishmonger; purchasing fish in the afternoon invited digestive distress, in my experience. Fate, however, had different plans for me.

Outside the fishmonger's, some young boys were throwing rocks at something and laughing. I saw that it was a frightened young gray and white tabby cat, no longer a kitten but not fully grown. The poor thing was very thin, and very scared. I handed the basket to Erik and strode up to the brats.

"Leave it alone!" I raised my voice in ire. "It's done nothing to you. Leave it be!"

The urchins scattered, but not without calling a few oaths in their wake. I squatted down and called to the cat, wiggling my fingers enticingly. Eventually, it -- he, as I soon noticed -- came over to me. A bit more crooning on my part, and he rubbed his face on my hand and began to purr. I picked him up and cuddled him to me.

"You poor thing," I murmured into the top of his head. "No one's taking care of you, are they?"

I looked up at Erik; with a resigned expression, he went into the fishmonger's to buy something to feed the cat who was obviously going home with us. A couple more stops saw me pointing out that we needed bread, butter, and a bucket of milk; Erik went in to make the purchases so that I could hold the creature.

We walked home, the cat content to be snuggled in my arms.

"Well, my dear, it appears we now have a pet," Erik laughed. "What will you call him?"

"Pierre, I think. It just seems to fit him somehow."

When we reached the house, I put my purchases in the kitchen while Erik fetched wood for both stove and fireplace. Pierre amused himself by exploring all of the rooms, sniffing and rubbing his face on the furniture.

"Where will he ... er ... use the water closet?" Erik asked when he had stacked the wood.

I hadn't thought about that.

"Do you think he'll run away if I let him outside?" I asked, as I put a dish of milk on the floor next to the small plate of shredded fish. Pierre ate hungrily, purring all the while.

"I doubt that little fellow will go anywhere," Erik said

indulgently. "I happen to like cats very much, Claire. I think Pierre will be a grand pet for us." His smile was soft.

"I wonder, my dear, if you would start a fire in the fireplace?" I said as I put the dinner makings in the larder. "I'll be out in a moment."

As Erik laid the fire, I went into the bedroom and closed the door. I took off my new dress, brushed it carefully to remove the cat hair and dust from our visit into town, and put it in the armoire. I then removed my corset, shoes and stockings, and slipped into the lacy green silk peignoir set. I brushed my hair down over my shoulders and was just getting ready to turn from the mirror when Erik opened the door.

"The fire is started ...." He gasped as he took in my appearance. "Oh dear god, Claire. I think a fire is going to start in here as well."

"My darling husband," I said as I crossed the room, "I wonder if you would care to join me on the chaise in the parlor." I caressed his arm as I passed by, with a look over my shoulder that made my intentions quite plain.

It took Erik a few minutes to join me. When he did appear in the parlor, he was wearing only loose silk trousers; his mask and hairpiece were left behind in the boudoir along with his attire from the afternoon.

"I took the liberty of laying a fire in the kitchen stove," he said as he sat next to me. "We'll want to eat those filets eventually."

As he made no move to touch me, I laid a hand on his arm.

"Erik, is something wrong?"

He turned to face me full-on.

"I don't understand how you could have agreed to look at this face every day for the rest of your life," he replied quietly.

I stood up from the chaise. "Lie down here," I requested.

When he had done as I asked, I knelt next to the chaise and caressed his face, touching the port-wine stained cheek and damaged bone with a light hand. I was still afraid of causing pain because the skin there seemed so delicate. He leaned into my touch and dropped a kiss on my inner wrist.

"Because, Erik LeMaitre, my husband, I love this face with all of my heart. Behind this face is the heart and soul of a poet, a knight."

I placed my mouth on his then, gently at first, and then with greater ardor as Erik's fingers entwined themselves in my hair.

CHAPTER 22

From the pages of Erik's journal:

I write these lines as I watch my wife sleep. She is wrapped in a coverlet and curled up on the chaise longue, with her new cat purring in the crook of her knees.

My wife. I cannot help but wonder whether I will ever grow accustomed to that phrase. As the Bard wrote, marriage is an honor I had dared not dream.

I don't know whether it was my imagination, but our lovemaking tonight felt more tender than usual and yet more sure and settled at the same time. Every touch of Claire's hands on my skin inflames my ardor. I cannot imagine how I lived before I met her.

The simple pleasure of doing the marketing together amazed me. I don't know that I would have dared to do so without her there. I will admit that the traveling fair's presence, though abhorrent on many levels, gave me the freedom to go into the shops. No one questions an oddity when the town is temporarily filled with them.

After our lovemaking, Claire insisted on making our supper; the simple fare was delicious. Then, I read to her for a while and she fell asleep on the chaise. I brought the quilt from the foot of the bed and covered her with it.

I am amazed to find myself the object of a woman's desire, nay, her ardor. I am beyond delighted that she accepted my proposal when she could so easily have gainsaid my advances. Just thinking about her passionate lovemaking stirs my body with desire.

For now, though, I am content to watch her sleep.

I awoke the next morning in the bedroom, where I distinctly did not recall going! I subsequently learned that Erik had carried me in from the parlor and tucked me in before retiring himself. My husband was already up and about, and came into the room when he heard me stirring. I donned a warm wrapper and was brushing my hair when he sat down on the bed with the newspaper in his hand.

"My love, I've been reading *Le Matin*," he began.

"You bought *Le Matin* here?" I interrupted, surprised that a Paris paper was available in the small village.

"Yes, I did. Please, look at this article." He held out the paper, folded open to a specific story, and I took it.

As I read the article, I gaped in astonishment. The story concerned Giraud's murder, which had been ruled as death by misadventure and the inquest closed since no real cause of death could be determined. I had known Erik's weapon was effective, but had no idea up until then just how skilled he was in its use. I could not suppress a shiver. I was further amazed that my name was mentioned insofar as I had disappeared. However, the description Francois had given of me was so significantly divorced from reality that no one would ever identify me by it.

"Tall, with golden hair?" I laughed. "I am neither of those things."

Erik was more solemn.

"It could mean any number of things, but I suspect Dupin and

Richard have paid your cousin handsomely to remain silent on the matter. Those two fools cannot afford any further scandal attached to their opera house. This does not, however, mean that your cousin will not attempt to find you himself. I'm very concerned that this might be the case."

I sat down next to him on the bed. "Well, what do you mean to do then?"

"Right now? I intend to enjoy the remainder of our honeymoon. When we return to Paris, we will decide together what to do. Shall we break our fast, my love?"

He stood and walked out of the room.

For a man determined to enjoy the remainder of our honeymoon, Erik was in a very black funk indeed. He barely spoke as I made tea and toast, and we ate our first breakfast as man and wife in uncomfortable silence.

I cleared the dishes from the table and washed them before returning to the bedroom to complete my toilette for the day. When I entered the water closet, I found that Erik had put in a dirt box for Pierre so that the cat would not have to go outside. Said cat was happily curled up on the bed asleep.

After a quick wash-up using hot water from the tea kettle mixed with cold water from the sink pump, I dressed in a simple dark skirt and blouse and pinned my hair up. I was pinning the straw bonnet in place when Erik came into the bedroom.

"I'm going into town to do the day's marketing," I said. "Do you wish to accompany me."

"No," he replied quietly. "Go on without me." He sat down on the bed with his back to me.

"Are you sure?"

"Just go, Claire."

I had no idea what I'd done to cause offense and, in fact, could think of nothing untoward that had occurred. This made me somewhat irate, to say the least.

"Very well then, Monsieur. You are welcome to sit here in the house for the remainder of the day. I, on the other hand, will be out and about getting to know the shopkeepers in town."

With that, I gathered my reticule and marketing basket and stalked out of the house.

CHAPTER 23

From the pages of Erik's journal:

I am, as the Bard would say, Fortune's fool.

How can I tell her? I am learning just how much I do not know about human interactions. I don't know how to tell Claire that I am worried about her safety without somehow insulting her independence. And yet, I have obviously done exactly that. My own foolish pride stopped me from following her to the door and calling after her: begging her to wait and offering to accompany her. How can I right the wrong I have done by saying nothing?

There is still time for me to catch up to her. I will join her after all.

I was close to tears as I made my way into town. My hands trembled and I was sure I did not present a very pleasant picture to the local villagers doing their marketing. I fought back the tears and planned what I would purchase: some carrots, *petit pois*, a chicken, some chicken stock. More bread and perhaps a pot of jam or honey. Fish for Pierre.

I also felt a trifle lightheaded and too warm, both of which I put down to not enough breakfast and too much anger.

I was momentarily sidetracked by a bookseller's window. My mind harkened back to the night before, with Erik reading to me in the parlor. I loved everything about him, but his mellifluous voice was one of the things I adored the most.

I stepped into the bookseller's, inhaling the peculiar smell of old paper and glue that seemed to permeate such establishments. The elderly, bespectacled gentleman proprietor nodded a greeting to me and I browsed the shelves. I found a chair, where I sat down when I had another bout of lightheadedness, which made paging through the books very convenient. I chose a couple of novels and a small volume of poems and paid for my selection. My purchases were wrapped in brown paper by the gentleman, who bade me return and wished me good day. I would, if nothing else, look forward to reading my new acquisitions.

I crossed over to the greengrocer's to select my carrots and peas, and it was then I noticed my husband at the flower stand. As always, the beauty of his unmarred left side took my breath away. What a rakehell he would have been but for an accident of birth, I thought. The flower girl was obviously charmed and intrigued by him. His porcelain mask leant an air of mystery to him and, with his flawless manners and elegant bearing, he might have been a nobleman.

Erik looked up the street and caught my eye, hurrying toward me with a beautiful nosegay of roses.

"Claire," he said, "I am so sorry."

"For what?" I asked. "Clearly I am the one who has caused offense somehow."

"No, my god, no," he whispered, his eyes closed. When he opened them, they shone with emotion. "I am worried about you. After all we have seen, I fear that your cousin will find you and do you harm; I could not live through losing you."

I stood there as though moonstruck, the vegetables forgotten.

"Do you really think such a thing might occur?"

He nodded.

"Well, don't let's think about it for now. Like you, I want to enjoy the rest of our time in the country. Now, won't you help me by going to the charcuterie for a chicken and some stock?"

He lifted my hand to his mouth and brushed my knuckles with his lips. "Anything you want."

Erik met me on the sidewalk with the package from the butchers' and added it to my basket full of vegetables, jam and sundries. We stopped at the fishmongers' for Pierre and, when the last item was packed into the basket, Erik carried it as we walked back to the cottage.

"I wish you had just told me this morning," I said. "I can't tell what you are thinking, you know."

As Erik unlatched the door, I made him promise that he would always tell me when he was worried about something.

I felt quite tired from my exertions, which was surprising. I went into the bedroom to loosen my stays a bit, as I felt even warmer than before. La grippe had gone around my Place des Vosges neighborhood, and I suspected I had a slight touch of it. What a splendid way to spend a honeymoon, I groaned inwardly.

"Erik," I called, "could you come into the boudoir?"

Something in my tone must have told him that I did not have passion in mind, because when Erik entered the room, his look was one of concern. Finding me in skirt and stays, the back loosened, did not help.

"What is it?"

"In all of the finery you purchased for me, is there a flannel night rail? I don't recall seeing one. I feel rather poorly ..."

His face solemn, Erik felt my forehead. "You've a fever."

Erik ransacked the clothespress and turned up beautiful lawn and silk nightwear but nothing warm. He opened his own drawers and pulled out a linen shirt and the loose silk trousers he favored for nightwear.

"Put these on," he insisted. "I'll go into town and get you a flannel night rail myself if you want, but first we need to get you out of those clothes and into bed." He smiled then. "God help me, this may be the first time I've wanted you in bed without thoughts of lovemaking."

"And this may be the first time since I've known you in which such thoughts are absent from my own wicked head," I laughed drily as I sat down on the bed to remove my shoes and stockings.

"No, let me." Erik removed my shoes, stockings and garters efficiently and then bade me stand up so that he could untie the waist of my skirt and remove my corset. The sheer lawn chemise was unbuttoned and dropped to the floor and Erik helped me into his elegant linen shirt, which hung to my knees. The silk trousers were, of course, too long and the waist large on me; fortunately, they had a drawstring that could be tightened.

"You look charming," he said as I looked down at the absurd costume whilst tugging the pins out of my hair.

"Please, Claire, just let me."

Erik sat me down on the bed again and took the remaining pins out of my hair. He brushed it efficiently, braided it into a loose plait, helped me under the covers and fluffed the pillows.

"I believe I saw some books in that basket; I'll be back in a moment to read to you."

When he returned, Erik had not only a book but a large glass of water.

"Sip from this," he said. "Don't try to drink too quickly."

Pierre hopped up on the bed to curl up next to me, purring loudly as Erik pulled up the chair from the vanity up next to me. The little heart-backed chair hardly seemed as though it would accommodate Erik's frame, but somehow he managed. Even now, I noticed that he seated himself with his left side facing toward me. Through my fever's fog, I wondered how long it would take him to understand that I cared for more than his looks.

Erik perused the titles I had chosen.

"Hmmm. Balzac's 'Passion in the Desert' seems a little much just at this time," he mused. "Perhaps a few selections from the Bard's 'Sonnets' instead."

He read aloud to me, his beautiful voice lulling me into a state of relaxation and, eventually, sleep.

I was awakened later by a metallic crash, and a curse from the other room.

"Damn you, you accursed cat! Continue in this way and you'll be made into violin strings!"

I got out of bed and went into the kitchen to see what was the matter.

CHAPTER 24

I found Erik shooing Pierre away as he cut up the chicken we'd bought earlier in the day. Pierre had jumped up on the draining board and knocked down the roasting pan lid. Erik looked so annoyed that I could not restrain a giggle.

"Ah! You're awake," he said. "I hope chicken roasted with potatoes and carrots will be adequate. I've also included some rosemary and lavender from the garden."

I must have goggled as I sat down at the small table.

"Yes, my dear, I do know how to prepare dishes other than eggs," he continued. "However, I ordinarily do so without the assistance of a cat."

Pierre jumped up into my lap and Erik was then able to finish his cookery and put the pan into the oven.

After he washed his hands, Erik came over and touched my forehead.

"Still feverish. I suspect a touch of la grippe."

I nodded in agreement; I felt miserable.

"Here," he said, pouring some hot liquid from a pot into a mug for me. "It's an infusion of white tea and lavender. The lavender will help bring down your fever, and also help you to sleep."

I sipped obediently at the steaming liquid and was surprised to find it quite tasty.

"Where did you learn about this?" I asked.

"In Persia."

The subject was clearly closed, because Erik walked out of the kitchen and into the parlor, only to return with a parcel wrapped in brown paper.

"I hope this will meet your needs," he said as he put it into my lap. "While you slept, I had plenty of time to go into town."

"Really? How long have I been asleep?"

Erik examined his pocket watch. "Some three hours."

I untied the string around the parcel and opened it to find a soft flannel night rail, printed with lavender flowers and pintucked at the bodice.

"There were some with lace, but the quality was poor and it was itchy," Erik said quietly as he took the chair opposite me. "I thought you would like this one."

I realized that he was unsure of how this plain gift would be received, but I was touched by his thoughtfulness.

"Thank you so much, my love. You do look out for me." I reached across the table and caressed his hand. He smiled then, obviously reassured.

"We have nearly an hour before supper will be ready," he said. "Why don't you change out of my clothes and into your night gown, and then come into the parlor."

I went into the bedroom and did as he asked. The gown was a little long, but that meant I'd be able to tuck my feet underneath. I undid my braid, brushed my hair out, and tied it loosely at my neck with a length of lavender ribbon. The soft cotton flannel was warm and comforting against my skin.

When I came into the parlor, I found that Erik had built a fire there and laid featherbeds on the chaise.

"Please relax here," he said. "I'll see to your needs."

The steaming mug of lavender tea was on a table next to the chaise, and I drank the draught greedily.

From the pages of Erik's journal:

I have always been blessed with good health, save for the circulation problem that plagues me with cold hands in winter. Claire, fortunately, is a hale and hearty soul, for I know that people die of la grippe. If my travels brought me nothing else, I have learned enough herb lore to know what will help her. Fortunately, many of the things I need are right in Zareh's garden.

She looks surprisingly pretty in the night gown I bought for her in town, the lavender lighting her blue eyes. A simple thing, and yet precisely what was needed. The happiness in her eyes, so bright in a face pale with fever, was worth the agony of going into town alone and enduring the stares at my mask.

I kept her wrapped in blankets before the fire, for I know that the fever is her body's way of trying to warm itself. I plied her with the lavender tea, which she fortunately enjoys. I brought her a plate with a small serving of chicken and vegetables, encouraging her to eat something although she had little appetite. Now, she is asleep on the chaise longue, her tabby cat curled in the crook of her knees.

I find myself angry at her illness, of all things. Not angry at Claire for falling ill, but at the illness itself. We should be celebrating our honeymoon together ... with all that is implied there. Yet, this illness has taken that time from us both. I will make it up to her, I vow it.

CHAPTER 25

I woke the next morning to Erik's gentle kiss on my forehead. He was kneeling, barefaced, next to the chaise. When I caressed his ravaged cheek, it was rough with stubble. His clothes were disheveled; he had obviously remained awake all night.

"Good morning, my love," I whispered.

"Good morning," he smiled. "Your fever has decreased somewhat; you feel cooler to the touch. I want you to remain quiet today, and continue drinking the lavender tea."

I nodded my assent, even as I put my arms around his neck and drew him to me. I kissed him gently.

"I promise to be a very good patient, Monsieur le Docteur. I'll drink the tea until it comes out my ears if it will please you. But you, my darling Erik, are the greatest tonic I know. You didn't need to stay up with me."

"And what if you had needed something in the night?" he asked. "I needed to be there for you."

I sat up on the chaise and pushed the featherbeds away. I stood up, but felt lightheaded and sat back down. Erik was on his feet immediately.

"Just tell me what you need and I'll bring it to you, Claire."

I laughed a little then.

"I do not think you can bring the water closet, my love."

"Ah. No ... but I can help you to it."

I stood again and took his arm, and he walked me to the necessary room. I felt silly, but had to admit to myself that I was rather weak and that the assistance was appreciated. I glanced at myself in the mirror; my face was wan, my eyes ringed in dark circles. I shook my head in disgust at my reflection and then allowed Erik to help me back to the parlor.

"I look dreadful," I sighed as I sank onto the chaise.

"Then we are indeed a pair," Erik said drily, rubbing his chin. I could hear the stubble rasp against his hand.

"I would love a bath," I sighed. "I do wish we had your *caldarium* right now."

Erik sat down next to me and caressed my cheek, tilting my chin up toward him.

"Claire, you are beautiful in my eyes now, and always." He kissed me again and then smiled. "I have some very happy memories of that *caldarium* thanks to you."

I stroked his cheek again, and he leaned into my palm to kiss the inside of my wrist. I shivered with pleasure, as he knew I would. I leaned against his chest and sighed with contentment and happiness.

"Claire," Erik began, "I had a thought last night which I think we should discuss." He paused, as though deciding how to proceed.

"Go on," I replied, looking up at him.

"Would you consider leaving France?"

"I would go anywhere with you, Erik. Why do you ask?"

"Just a thought at this point, my love."

I sensed that this was not the entire truth, and said so.

He sighed then. "Am I so transparent?"

Erik reached over to the table where he had left a newspaper.

"I purchased this yesterday when I went into town. I think you should read this." Erik indicated a segment in the agony column as he handed me the paper. I read, astonished, at the item my cousin Francois had entered offering a reward for information that would allow him to find me.

"I don't believe in running away, Erik," I said.

"Nor, my love, do I. However, I cannot like this after all that we saw in your dressing room. It was this newspaper item, more than anything else, that kept me wakeful all last night. Wakeful, Claire, with worry." His eyes were bright with emotion.

I shuddered, remembering the scene Erik and I had witnessed through the two-way mirror.

"There is only one thing I wish to do right now," I said. "And that is to have a bath. Other decisions can wait."

I went into the kitchen and pumped cold water into kettles for boiling. It had been a long while since I'd done this chore myself; I was quite spoiled by the water boys who brought the tub to my room at the opera house. Hot water drawn from the boilers was just the right temperature for bathing by the time it got to me. This would be a much longer process.

"Would you let me, please?" Erik said as I started to pull the brass tub into the parlor before the fireplace. He lifted it easily, and lined it with a sheet so that the heat from the metal wouldn't burn my skin.

"Just sit," he said as I went back into the kitchen to get cold water to put into the tub.

I groaned at his insistence, but ultimately let him take care of the matter. It was certainly easier than arguing.

Erik poured some of the warm water from my kettle into a pitcher and went into the bedroom. I followed him and sank down on the bed as he poured the water into a basin. He stripped off his disheveled shirt next, and then soaped his face and shaved. After completing his ablutions, Erik laid down next to me on the bed and kissed me.

"Better?" he asked, taking my hand and laying it against his cheek.

"Oh yes," I breathed, and reached to kiss him hungrily.

"None of that just yet, dear," he said, although his voice was husky with desire.

We each heaved a little sigh then, and went back into the parlor. Erik poured the hot water into the tub, testing the temperature before helping me in. I washed quickly, not taking my usual time luxuriating in the bath. It felt wonderful to have self and hair clean again.

Erik handed me a towel as I stood up from the tub and I dried hurriedly as I made my way back to the bedroom. There was a part of me that wished for a fireplace in that room as well, so that we did not go back and forth so much. On the other hand I was grateful to Zareh for lending us his little cottage. I was just so tired from feeling ill.

I combed my damp hair and then toweled it again until it was almost dry; a quick brushing finished the job. I folded the towel and placed it at the foot of the very inviting bed and crawled, nude, under the featherbeds and settled onto the pillows. The fine lawn sheets felt wonderful against my skin. I would just close my eyes for a moment, I thought.

CHAPTER 26

Erik awoke me with a gentle caress; his touch against my bare skin was like fire and I moaned as I reached for him. I entangled my fingers in his hair, still slightly damp from his own bath, as he set his lips to the base of my throat.

"My love," he whispered, over and over, his lips brushing my skin at random. First a shoulder, then my throat again, then a brief touch on the swell of my bosom. My desire mounted into an ardor that would have embarrassed a more modest woman than myself. When at last he entered me, I shamelessly wrapped my legs around his waist and pulled him in deeper. I licked and nibbled at his chest, raking my nails across his shoulders. The sounds issuing from my throat seemed more animal than human, so consumed was I with wanting him.

All too soon, our lovemaking reached its crescendo. Erik settled next to me, his damaged cheek again hidden in the pillow so that only the unmarred left side was visible.

"Oh, Claire," he whispered. "If only you knew how much I love you."

"And I love you," I replied, kissing him. "Now, why don't you sleep? You were awake all night."

"Only if you stay with me."

"I shall," I promised, and settled into the crook of his arm.

I awoke again some time later. Erik's even breathing told me that he was sound asleep, for which I was grateful. I slipped out of bed, put on a wrapper, and sat down on the vanity chair to read. I could not concentrate on the pages, though; my mind was wandering entirely too much.

I glanced over at the bed. Erik had shrugged the featherbeds down in his sleep. He was lying on his belly and his scarred back was completely exposed. Unbidden, I began to cry silent tears; I could not bear cruelty in any form. I was unable to even imagine what his life had been like. Zareh had told me some little bit, and Erik had told me only slightly more. Overall, he was remarkably closed-mouthed about the horrors of his past.

I went into the kitchen and minced some of the leftover chicken into a bowl for Pierre. I looked into the larder to see what I might prepare for luncheon without going into town; Erik's wish that I should remain quiet today was a sound one.

In the other room, Erik began to cry out. I closed the larder and went back to the bedroom to see what was wrong. I realized instantly that he was in the throes of a nightmare; he had pushed the featherbeds entirely to the floor and was making the most anguished sounds I'd ever heard.

Then, the words that froze my heart: "Christine, don't go. I love you!"

I knew that one could hardly help one's dreams, much less one's nightmares. Nonetheless, an arrow of jealousy found its mark in my heart. How could I have been so foolish as to believe, after an absurdly short acquaintance and courtship, regardless of how long I had cared for his horse and secretly been watched by him, that I had supplanted the beautiful young soprano in his affections?

I stood, twisting the belt of my wrapper in my fingers, as the tears streamed down my face. I sat on the edge of the bed and tried to decide what to do next, but my thoughts were entirely too muddled.

Erik's thrashings calmed and his breathing became more steady as I sat there weeping. I don't know exactly when he awoke, or how long he watched me before he spoke.

"Claire, what is the matter?"

"Don't you know?" I asked quietly.

"No, Claire, I don't." He looked around at the bedclothes, which were all tangled, and then sighed. "Another of my nightmares, I suppose, the which I never remember. Did I frighten you, Claire?"

"Only once," I rejoined, and turned to look at him. "When you called out for Christine and told her that you loved her."

His green-gold eyes held my gaze steadily as he responded.

"That was a lifetime ago, Claire."

He slipped out of bed and went through my clothespress to find a handkerchief. While he was up, he donned the loose silk trousers he favored, and then knelt in front of me.

"Please, dry your eyes," he requested. His voice was low and gentle.

I took the handkerchief and did as he asked. He remained before me as though in supplication, and then laid his head in my lap. I stroked his raven-black hair and we sat in silence for a time.

At length, Erik spoke again. "I did love her, Claire. I think half the world knows that, after what I did on stage. Then she humiliated me. She was beautiful and talented, to be sure, but she was also a child. She was never really mine to love; I understand that now. After she left to marry that boy, the vicomte, I resigned myself to being alone for the rest of my days."

He stood up then and sat next to me on the bed, wrapping an arm around my waist.

"And then," he continued, "I saw this woman. Not a child, but a woman. She was different. She was a beauty of a different sort, and very kind. She obviously loved animals as much as I do. I began to watch her as I had once watched a little soprano, in secret, for I now truly feared to show my hideous face again."

I looked up at him and made to speak, but he laid a finger across my lips.

"Pray, let me finish." He drew a breath. "I never would have shown myself to you, Claire, had I not been afraid for your life that evening when your cousin wanted you to ride that Andalusian. Later, finding out that they had hurt him to make him dangerous to you made me angry. They hurt an innocent animal, and tried to kill you.

"Hearing you talk about your late fiance's injuries made me bold. I thought to myself that if you could love a man so badly burned, perhaps you would at least be my friend. I never dreamed that you would allow me to kiss you that day in the carriage, but my heart has been yours to command ever since."

Erik sighed deeply and dropped a gentle kiss on my forehead.

"Now, madame, I really must insist that you get back into bed and rest a little longer. I don't think you're quite past this illness just yet."

"You were the one who roused me, husband," I smiled. "In more ways than one."

His laugh was deep and throaty as I slipped between the covers.

"Shall I read to you again? Or would you prefer to play at cards?"

I opted for the card game and so we passed another pleasant hour of the morning before Erik went into town to procure supper. I amused myself with playing numerous games of Patience while I awaited his return. Pierre cuddled up next to me, so I didn't feel lonely at all.

When Erik did return some little while later, he came in to check on me immediately. When he found me reading to myself, and my fever decreased a little further, his relief was palpable.

"I sent a letter to Zareh while I was in the village," he informed me. "I've asked him to see to liquidating some of my holdings and transferring the funds to a bank in England."

I must have looked very surprised indeed.

"My dear," he informed me solemnly, "In the course of my travels I have acquired both money and property. I'm a very wealthy man. At the moment, I have more need of liquid assets than of property to which I will never return."

"So, your plan is for us to go to England, then?"

"Yes. The more I have considered it, the more I want for us to go somewhere new, where we can have a life together unfettered by my past."

"How fortunate for you then, my love, that I am what Francois always called an overeducated chit," I laughed. "I speak English fairly well." I did not point out that, no matter where we went, Erik could not escape his past; there seemed to be no point in doing so.

"As do I," Erik responded in that language, without a trace of his native French accent.

He turned more solemn then. "I saw your cousin in the village, Claire. It appears that he has brought the troupe here for a show or two. I think you should remain indoors until they have gone."

"Erik, I am no coward. Nor will I be kept prisoner for fear that I run into Francois." My tone was petulant, and I knew it. However, I would brook no resistance. "I will go to market and the like; I'll not hide myself."

Erik sighed with resignation. "I assumed you would say as much."

"Did you." There was no question in my tone.

"Yes, my love, I did. I've sent a note to Francois, asking that he meet me at the public house in the village tonight. I said in my message that I had information about you; that should assure his presence. When we meet, I will give him whatever funds he asks to leave us alone. I am not unwilling to resort to bribery for our peace of mind."

Erik's long, elegant fingers toyed with a slender gut rope that he pulled from a pocket. "Nor am I unwilling to resort to force again."

"God in heaven, Erik," I sighed. "Haven't there been enough killings already? If you must meet with my idiot cousin, promise that you won't do him physical harm."

I could see his reluctance, but he acquiesced at last.

We consumed a cold supper in uncomfortable and unaccustomed silence. At length, Erik rose from the table and donned his coat and hat.

"Please just stay here until I return," he insisted. "I shan't be long."

CHAPTER 27

I amused myself by playing with Pierre and reading for a time. However, after three hours passed I became concerned. I could not imagine what was taking so long. I decided to go into town to see for myself what had happened, Erik's concerns be damned. I changed from my wrapper to a plain blue wool dress and was just pinning my hair up when a loud knock came at the cottage door.

I looked out the window but could only see a man, in profile, holding a lantern.

"Mademoiselle Claire," the man called, "are you inside?"

I recognized the voice. Gilbert Rochambeau was my cousin's valet, and a gentle soul. One of his shoes had a built-up sole because the leg on that side was shorter; it had been broken and badly set. Francois never let Gilbert forget that he was not like other men because of his injury. I had not thought until quite recently how very cruel my cousin could be; I had been so swathed in my grief that I could only make certain of my own kindness. All the same, I could only surmise that Gilbert's presence boded no good. How could he possibly know where I was?

"Mademoiselle Claire," Gilbert called again. "I am come from a man who says he is your husband. I am come to help. As God is my judge, Mademoiselle, I am alone."

I opened the door a crack.

"Prove to me you came from Erik," I said quietly.

"God in heaven, Mademoiselle Claire. Er, Madame; it is all true then." His voice was rough with emotion.

Gilbert slipped his hand through the gap at the door, making no attempt to push further inside, and held his palm open. In it were Erik's wedding ring -- and a shard of the porcelain mask.

I opened the door the rest of the way and let Gilbert in.

"Where is he?" I demanded, pulling a shawl around my shoulders.

"Madame Claire, I promise you. I am come to help."

"So you have said, Gilbert. Now, answer me."

Gilbert hung his head. As usual, he looked dusty, dishevelled and miserable. "Francois has him locked in a stall in the stable tent. Madame Claire, you were always so kind to me. And now, I see the man whom you have married ... you love him? Even with such a face as that?"

"With all my heart, Gilbert."

"Then I am your man, Madame." Gilbert's tone was resolute. "I will help you and your husband. I only wish that I had never met your cousin, as I see the kind of man he truly is."

"Gilbert, if you help Erik and me, I promise you that you will not have to endure Francois' employment any further." Erik would need a valet in England, I reasoned; two birds might be killed with the same stone.

With that, Gilbert escorted me out the door. He was as good as his word; we were alone.

We walked in silence to the village square and into the traveling fair's environs. The majority of sound came from the far end of the green and it was there that we made our quiet way. I could hear my cousin's voice above the murmur.

"Come and see the monster who claims he married a lady," he called out in drunken tones. "This *thing* says he married my lovely cousin Claire, who has conveniently disappeared. Perhaps he has her stashed in his closet, like one of Bluebeard's wives."

Loud, vicious laughter greeted my cousin's remarks. Gilbert and I slipped into the midst of a crowd that consisted primarily of performers, some still in their spangled costumes. I pulled my shawl up to cover my hair and hide my face a little. I needed to see, but wished to remain unseen as much as possible.

Francois had locked Erik in one of the traveling stallion boxes: a sturdy cage. The look on Erik's unmasked face was one of feral fury, barely even human. His shirt was torn, the scars on his back visible through the ruined fabric. His hair had been raked through by frantic fingers, for it was loose around his cheeks instead of his usual pomaded coif. The remains of his broken porcelain mask were scattered on the ground in front of the stallion box. Yet Erik stood erect, proud and silent, in the face of his tormentor. This was obviously not at all new to him, and I better understood his abhorrence of traveling fairs.

"There are many here, milord, to whom my cousin Claire is well known," Francois mocked, taking a draught from a jug of whisky. "Tell them again how our little horsewoman loves you and your hideous face."

Erik maintained his stoic silence, only the muscle pulsing in his left cheek betraying the depth of his temper.

"Why doesn't he say or do anything," Gilbert whispered to me.

"Because," I responded, "I made him promise there would be no violence."

"Madame, you did not make *me* promise that," Gilbert responded.

I silenced him with a motion of my hand.

"Show us your wedding ring, you foul beast," Francois continued. "You were quite proud of it earlier when you said you were claiming your right as her husband."

Erik's hands were clearly visible, all of the elegant fingers bare. The crowd jeered yet again.

"Oh dear," Francois went on. "You seem to have lost your little bauble in all of the confusion."

Gilbert pressed Erik's ring into my hand. I slipped it into my reticule and maintained my silence. He gave me a questioning look, and I shook my head again.

"Since the thing won't speak, perhaps it will sing for us," Francois crowed. "I vaguely recall seeing this masked visage around the Opera Garnier. I cannot imagine what kind of hideous tones would issue from that face, but surely you will indulge us with your croaking tones."

Erik broke his silence then. His beautiful, clear tenor shocked the throng into silence, moving some to tears. The hypnotic power of his instrument was palpable as he brought his aria to a close and resumed his silent stance.

One woman near me remarked, "It's a bloody shame that he should have such a voice with that poor face of his. He sings like an angel."

The silent crowd began to disperse at that point. Francois took another draught from his jug and spat it at Erik's feet. He gestured to a nearby young woman and walked away with his arm around her shoulders.

Gilbert and I had moved into the shadows of another tent as the throng left the area and soon we were watching Erik by ourselves. Now that there was no audience, he began to pace the stall like an impatient lion in a zoo.

Gilbert made his way to the cage.

"I am returned, monsieur," he said quietly. "I have brought Madame Claire."

"You idiot," Erik hissed. "How could you endanger her that way? I wanted her merely to know where I was."

"He could not have stopped me," I responded as I stepped out of the shadows.

I drew Erik's wedding band from my reticule then. He slipped a trembling left hand through the stall's bars and I placed it on his finger just as I had done in the chapel on our wedding day.

"I do not have the key to this lock, monsieur, but if Madame Claire will give me one of her hairpins I will have it open in moments."

I tugged a pin from my braid and handed it to Gilbert, who was as good as his word. Erik had just stepped out of the stall and wrapped his arms around me, breathing raggedly, when Francois returned.

"Why, Claire, how lovely of you to join us," he slurred. "So, what this beast told us is true, eh? You have actually wed this malformed creature? When you could have had me?"

The horror must have shown on my face. "Come now, lovely cousin. Surely this is what your father had in mind when he gave me charge of your affairs in his will. You can annul your marriage with this creature and come with me."

"There can be no annulment," Erik said.

"Don't be ridiculous," Francois laughed drunkenly. "Of course it can be annulled."

"No, Francois, it cannot," I responded. "The marriage has been consummated."

"Impossible," Francois scoffed. "If it is true, though, I regret that you will so soon be made a widow." The sound of a butterfly knife unfolding made his meaning abundantly clear.

"And just so you can't repeat your little Punjabi trick, I took the liberty of relieving you of your gutstring when I relieved you of your coat, monsieur," he chortled drily.

The next sound was one of small arms fire. A red stain blossomed on Francois' shirtfront and he dropped to his knees with a shocked look on his face. Gilbert had drawn a small over-and-under derringer from his pocket, taken careful and deadly aim, and silenced my cousin forever.

CHAPTER 28

From the pages of Erik's Journal:

Now that Claire has ceased fussing about me and is asleep with the cat, I am able to write about what happened.

I promised Claire that I would do no harm, but I carried my Punjab lasso in a coat pocket anyway. I feel naked without its protection. I made my way to the public house and waited for Francois to arrive.

When he did come, he was not alone; this possibility had not occurred to me. Nevertheless, I beckoned for him to join me. His companions sat at another table, keeping an eye on the proceedings.

"So," he said to me. "What do you know of my cousin Claire?"

"She is safe," I rejoined. "She wants you to leave her alone, now and forever. I am prepared right now to pay any sum that you deem necessary in order to accomplish that end."

He laughed in my face. "By what right do you come here with this preposterous idea?"

I drew the glove slowly from my left hand so that he could see my ring. "By the right of a husband."

His surprise was genuine, then his tone became sly and mean.

"So, the little minx took a husband at last. You do know, of course, that you weren't her first. She was engaged once before, probably her last chance, but the poor sod died after a fire. Not because of his burns, of course, though that would have been a blessing. Drank laudanum rather than marry the cold bitch, you know."

I felt the muscle in my left cheek pulse; this happened every time I struggled to govern my temper. Francois' retelling of the sad end to which Claire's fiancé Philippe had come was both mean-spirited and dishonest.

Francois barked out another little laugh.

"When she was part of our horse troupe, she started sleeping with one of the opera patrons, whoring around with a man who would take her places in his carriage and buy her fine clothes. Every woman has a price, apparently, even my virtuous cousin. In her case, it was furbelows. Have a care, monsieur, that she has not given you the pox."

The pulsing muscle in my cheek became more prominent.

"She was not whoring, monsieur," I responded quietly. "That man was myself."

"Hoho!" Francois crowed. "The little bitch was actually courting?"

"I suggest, monsieur, that you cease to speak of my wife in that fashion." I toyed with the Punjab lasso in my pocket but realized there were too many witnesses -- to say nothing of the promise I had made to Claire.

"Oh, monsieur, I am sorry. I had temporarily forgotten that you made a point of claiming your right as Claire's husband." He gestured to his cohorts. "Come over here, gentlemen, and meet the fine fellow who has taken our Claire's hand in matrimony."

I was quickly surrounded by Francois' men.

"And now, monsieur, let us take a walk away from this pub if you do not mind." Francois rose and two of his men hauled me to my feet, grasping my arms just above the elbow and herding me toward the door. "We will have a talk in a place of my choosing."

The two men at my side forced me to follow Francois' lead, and soon we found ourselves in the passage between two sets of stable tents. At that point, Francois turned on me and sunk his fist hard and deep in to my solar plexus. As I doubled over, his companions pulled my jacket down hard so that I could not move my arms and then joined their leader in his efforts. Soon my jacket was completely gone, and with it my lasso. My shirt was torn as I attempted to fight off the horde. Then, somehow, my mask was knocked free and shattered on the hard-trampled ground in front of me, even as I was driven to my knees and held there by rough hands. Some of Francois' men drew back as they saw the ruin that the mask had covered, but the man himself began to laugh.

"Monsieur, you amuse me greatly. You would have me believe that my cousin married you? That she willingly came to chapel with you? Does she know how hideous you are? Surely not."

I remained silent, trying to catch my breath and wondering whether my ribs were merely bruised or actually broken. Each inhalation was an agony.

"I have just the place for an animal like you," Francois stated baldly. He gestured toward the two men holding me on the ground and they dragged me to my feet. "You see, inhuman creatures like yourself, monsieur, need to be caged."

With that, I was shoved into that traveling stallion box and the door was padlocked behind me. God in heaven, to be caged again after so many years of freedom! It was almost more than I could bear. I sank down in a corner of my prison and wrapped my arms around my knees, just as I had done as a child. My eyes ached with the desire to shed tears of desperation, but I realized that doing so would prevent me from focusing on what might be done to better my situation.

After a couple of hours, darkness fell. At length, a man bearing a lantern came along the way and I called out to him. "Monsieur, could you please come closer? I would have a word with you."

The man came as requested, but cautiously. He was obviously shocked by my appearance, both in the ruin of my clothes and at my abhorrent visage. However, he remained.

"Yes, monsieur?"

"Is it possible that you knew Claire Delacroix, cousin of this troupe's leader?" I inquired.

"Yes, monsieur. I am Gilbert, her cousin's valet. Mademoiselle Claire was always kind to me when others were not." He gestured downward, and my gaze followed his hand; one of the man's shoes was built up to compensate for a leg significantly shorter than its fellow. "How do you know her?"

"She is my newly-wed wife, Monsieur. Could you possibly take a message to her?"

He nodded, but still looked cynical. I removed the wedding band from my hand and passed it through the bars to him. "Take this to her, along with one of those pieces of porcelain on the ground. Tell her you come from Erik."

I explained the location of the honeymoon cottage.

"This isn't some kind of trick, is it?" Gilbert asked suspiciously. "There're some here who find it amusing to play tricks on me."

I shook my head sadly. "I swear to you, I am being wholly

honest. That ring holds more value to me than the mere gold from which it is crafted, and I had thought never to remove it from my hand again. Please, go to Claire and tell her where I am."

Gilbert then left me alone, his lantern light moving ever more distant. I hoped I had not erred in trusting him.

When Francois returned, he brought a large band of performers from all over the fair. The evening show had just ended; many of the performers were still in their costumes. The man was well into his cups and began to spiel to all present that the monster before them claimed to be married to his cousin.

I rose and walked to the front of the cage, where I stood in silence. My hubris had brought me to this place, but I would not be cowed by the drunken fool's taunts. The crowd's laughter grew more raucous as Francois mocked me. His method turned on him, though, when he dared to suggest that I sing. My voice has always been the one true beauty about me, almost freakishly pure of tone and pitch. I chose an aria of which I was especially fond, and I sang: sang the crowd into silence and tears, as I had known I could.

When the crowd dispersed, Gilbert was there, and Claire with him. At first I was angry that Gilbert had endangered her, and then I realized that her stubbornness was matched only by my own. I was truly glad to see her. Gilbert picked the lock on the cage door and released me to Claire's waiting arms. We would have left quietly, but for Francois' ill-timed return ... and Gilbert's well-aimed pistol, which put an end to Francois' mockery once and for all.

We hurried down the alley between the stable tents, my breath ragged with the pain in my ribs. Claire's stride was purposeful and she looked from left to right at the stalls until she found the one she wanted.

"Gilbert, take Pierrot. Saddle him quickly and ride for Paris. Go to the Opera Garnier and find Madame Antoinette Giry. Tell her you are come from me. Ask her to take you to the daroga. When you are with the daroga, tell him he must send the coach for us as soon as possible," she stated briskly. "Tell him we will want to stay at the Place des Vosges townhouse until further arrangements can be made and that you will stay there as Erik's valet."

Gilbert nodded. "I will do as you ask, Madame. I promise."

Claire dug into her reticule and handed Gilbert some coins. "Money for the journey and your troubles, Gilbert. We will see you in Paris."

Gilbert sketched a bow to her and then went into the stall to saddle the black Andalusian. We, for our part, made our way quietly away from the town square and back toward the cottage. Our progress was slowed somewhat as Claire matched her stride to mine, and I am sorry to say that I had to lean on her more than a little at times because I was so sore.

When we were finally safe within the walls of the little house, Claire broke down in hysterical tears.

"Oh, god, Erik," she gasped as she dried her eyes, "I should not have let you go."

"And how, my dear, would you have prevented me?" My tone was far more dry than I intended.

She shook her head then. "I don't know. Now, tell me where your medicines are so that I can treat those bruises, and I'll bind your ribs."

I had no idea my wife could be such a cool customer. Not one word did she utter about her cousin, and she was very businesslike as she cut a pillowslip to serve as a makeshift wrap around my torso. Every bruise was besmeared with calendula and each cut daubed with witch-hazel.

When Claire finished her doctoring, she insisted that I be seated and have a cup of tea. As I sipped the same lavender infusion with which I had plied her, she gently stroked my hair. At length she whispered to me.

"I would die without you, Erik. You are my soul."

Her kiss fell gently on the ruin of my right cheek, and I could feel the warmth of her tears.

Before I got out my pen and journal, I knelt next to her, each movement reminding me that I was injured. I made a vow to my wife to always look after her and keep her safe from harm ... for she is my soul as well.

CHAPTER 29

While we waited for the coachman, Erik and I packed our belongings. My beautiful trousseau went back into the boxes, which were carefully tied shut. Erik's clothes went into a large valise. I managed to find a wicker picnic basket that would do to contain my new kitten; I was not about to abandon my pet.

While we were packing, I expounded on my idea of Erik taking Gilbert as his valet. He was slightly incredulous at the thought.

"He looks dusty and unkempt, Claire."

"Yes, Erik, he does, but Francois never did. Is that not the most important thing?"

My fastidious husband raised an eyebrow.

"Besides which," I argued, "He is helping us, down to committing murder on our behalf. Do you not think we owe him something? I certainly do."

"You are a stubborn minx, aren't you? Very well. I need a valet, and you need a majordomo. But we're going to do something about Gilbert's appearance when we get to Paris."

"Thank you, Erik. It's the right thing to do."

It would be at least two hours before Gilbert reached Paris, by my calculations. On horseback alone, he was faster than a coach, but Pierrot could not sustain a canter for thirty miles. Add another three hours, minimum, before Zareh's coach would collect us, I realized, and we would arrive in Paris midmorning. I said as much to Erik, knowing he wanted to avoid our being seen.

"We haven't much choice, Claire. We need to leave here as soon as possible. Now, let's try to get some sleep before the coach comes."

We laid down on the bed in our clothes, that we might be ready at once when help arrived.

I did not expect to doze off after the evening's excitement, but my husband's even breathing must have lulled me. I woke to Gilbert shaking my shoulder.

"Madame Claire, wake up. Your friend and I are come."

Indeed, Zareh had come for us himself.

"Hurry, my friends, and let us get these things atop the coach," he said with a gesture toward the boxes.

I left that to the men while I rounded up my protesting kitten and put him in the basket.

"Just for a while, mon ami. We will be home soon."

I went outside just as the last box was being secured. Zareh was in the coachman's seat and Gilbert took up the footman's spot. Erik helped me into the coach, where I settled Pierre's basket on the seat next to me.

"This was not the wedding trip I had imagined," Erik grimaced as he settled in across from me.

"Me either, I must admit. Yet, here we are." I tried to smile but the emotions of the past few days caught up with me at last. "Oh, Erik, what shall we do?"

"Continue with my plan to leave France as soon as possible. We will take Gilbert with us, of course; someone may have seen him shoot your cousin. And you are right; we are in his debt."

Other than my brief idyll as a schoolgirl in Switzerland, I had never lived outside of France. The Zurich boarding school had been like a tiny kingdom unto itself, and we students had not gone about unescorted. I had to admit to myself that living abroad sounded like a great adventure. When I said as much to Erik, he grew solemn.

"Claire, I lived away from France for many years. It is not an easy thing, being far from home."

"But we'll be together, Erik," I responded plaintively. "That's all that matters to me."

Erik just looked at me sadly. "Yes, Claire, and that is more comfort to me than you know."

CHAPTER 30

The rocking motion of the carriage made me drowsy, and I dozed on and off until we pulled up in front of the Place des Vosges townhouse. Antoinette Giry had been waiting for us there; she opened the door and nearly flew down the stairs to meet me.

"Claire, you must come inside and tell me what happened, my dear. The men will get your belongings."

I followed my friend inside and into the kitchen.

"I don't even know where to start, Antoinette. So many things have happened."

I opened Pierre's basket and let the kitten out to explore. He immediately stropped himself against Antoinette's black skirt, leaving a streak of white hair near the hem, and then ran around examining dark corners.

I removed my shawl and sank into a chair.

"I'll just start at the beginning," I sighed.

I finished relating the events since our wedding as Zareh, Gilbert and Erik trooped into the kitchen themselves. Antoinette made a pot of chocolate while I spoke, and we all partook of the warm, refreshing beverage.

"Madame Claire," Gilbert began, "Your husband has offered me a position as your majordomo. I don't know how to thank you."

Erik looked him up and down, taking in his dirty, disheveled clothes and shaggy hair.

"You can start by burning those clothes and having a bath and shave," he responded drily. "We'll proceed from there."

"I haven't any other clothes," Gilbert pointed out. "I left in something of a hurry."

"Yes, I suppose you did," Erik replied. "Stand in front of me."

He and Gilbert looked one another in the eye.

"Zareh," Erik said, turning to his friend, "Could you bring the rest of my clothes from your home? I have plenty of things that will fit our friend. And bring your valet; we'll need his barbering skills."

Zareh promised to return within the hour, and Antoinette made her good-byes as well. I showed Gilbert around the house and asked him to pick a room for his own. He asked for a room on the first floor, off the kitchen; the less he had to go up and down the stairs, the better for his leg. Erik and I would use the white and gold master bedroom.

Erik had pulled a jacket, waistcoat, shirt, cravat and trousers from his valise.

"These are for you, Gilbert. After you bathe."

Gilbert's eyes goggled at the costly attire.

"For me? I can't pay for those."

"Nor shall you. Consider them part of your salary."

"Yes, sir ... Monsieur Erik."

I was surprised that Gilbert's pride did not seem to be hurt at Erik's brusque behavior. On the other hand, my cousin had been far from kind to his valet; perhaps he did not notice anymore.

The townhouse had a beautiful bathroom with a deep claw-foot tub. Erik kept some of his sandalwood soap there, and I gave a bar to Gilbert along with some Turkish towels.

"Are you sure, Madame Claire? It's your bath. I should use a tub in the kitchen."

"Go on, Gilbert. It's fine." I turned on the taps and closed the door behind me.

I went down to the kitchen to tidy up the cups and chocolate pot. Erik was asleep on one of the chairs, as he had succumbed to exhaustion. I could not resist; his sinfully beautiful lips were too much of a temptation. I kissed him, more passionately than I intended.

"Mmmm," Erik groaned as his arms stole around my waist. "Hoyden."

"You bring it out in me," I whispered as I brushed my lips across his forehead.

"Madame Claire ... Monsieur Erik." Gilbert stood in the kitchen door, dressed in his new clothes. His hair was still wet from the bath, but the improvement in his appearance was remarkable.

"Gilbert, you look wonderful." My praise was sincere; I'd never noticed before how handsome he was. His hair, which had always seemed a dull brown, was a deep gold that offset his warm brown eyes. Dressed in Erik's clothes, he looked every inch the gentleman.

"Yes, my friend, much improved," Erik added. He rubbed a hand across his own stubbled cheek then. "We could both do with a barbering; luckily, we need not wait much longer.

Erik went to bathe then and Gilbert and I were alone in the kitchen. I felt uncomfortable all of a sudden, but could not say exactly why.

"Madame Claire," Gilbert said at last, "Why are you not looking at me?"

The truth was that I felt guilty. Gilbert had always been somewhat invisible to me. I'd been kind to him, but I'd never given much thought about what his life was like. Now I was keenly aware of him. He'd always been a handsome, kind man; it was just now that he wore a good suit of clothes that I could see it. I was possessed of no small amount of self-loathing at my own shallowness. I looked Gilbert in the eye, and said as much.

"Me? Handsome? With this leg?" He gestured again, not yet realizing that the cut and proper length of the trousers hid his disability from view. "You are too kind to me."

I was saved from replying by Zareh letting himself in the front door, valet in tow.

CHAPTER 31

I excused myself as Zareh's valet, Etienne, unpacked his barbering implements on the kitchen table. Erik had finished his bath and I hoped there was hot water left for me. Gratefully, I discovered that there was, and I sank into a tub of rose-scented water.

After scrubbing myself thoroughly and donning a fresh shirtwaist and skirt, I went back down to the kitchen. Etienne was finishing Erik's shave; snippets of black hair on the floor were evidence of a haircut. A touch of bay rum on his cheeks and macassar pomade to his hair completed the process. Erik donned his leather mask after brushing the last bits of hair from his sleeves.

"You next, Gilbert."

"I've always shaved myself and cut my own hair ..."

Etienne gestured toward the kitchen chair after cleaning and stropping the razor.

"Has no one ever done this for you?" I asked.

"No, madame."

"Then it is time, Gilbert. Let someone look after you for a change." I gestured again toward the chair, and Gilbert seated himself. Etienne fastened the cloth around his neck.

Gilbert's air of trepidation was palpable, and grew more apparent as scissors flashed and hair fell to the floor. A shave and pomade, and then a mirror; Gilbert was dumbfounded at his reflection.

Unlike Erik's hair, which was severely swept back from his brow, Gilbert's coif was a fashionable, close-cropped Caesar cut with a fringe that emphasized his eyes. He looked every inch the gentleman dandy. I wondered how I would keep the neighborhood soubrettes and ballet dancers from beating down the door to get at my majordomo.

Gilbert finally put down the mirror and stood up. He extended his hand to Erik.

"I ... thank you, Monsieur Erik. I don't know what to say."

Erik shook his hand. "My wife's majordomo should look like the gentleman he is."

Erik paid Etienne. Zareh had been reading the newspaper in the parlor and we all joined him there while his manservant tidied up and repacked his tools.

"Who is this gentleman?" Zareh smiled at Gilbert. "Surely this is not the man who disturbed my peace? He was a shabby creature, and before me stands a prince."

Gilbert swelled with pride. "I must look like a gentleman now, for Madame Claire."

Erik and I exchanged amused looks. Gilbert's very demeanor had changed before our eyes, and I sensed that I would have a very protective majordomo indeed.

CHAPTER 32

July 1889

It was a good thing that we lived on a square full of artistes and authors. Otherwise, scandal might have reigned as Madame LeMaitre went about with Rochambeau, the far too dashing majordomo. Gilbert accompanied me anywhere from Les Halles to the Louvre or the recently opened Eiffel Tower, and none of our neighbors turned a hair.

Zareh and Erik were often closeted away, making arrangements to move our tiny household to London. As part of that process, Erik gave me two items that rather surprised me: a bank account and traveling papers, both in my name ("Should anything happen to me, you'll not be destitute," he explained).

We worked daily on improving my English by reading Shakespeare's works, and even began to teach Gilbert. My accent came through no matter how hard I tried to emulate Erik's perfect diction, and there were times when I threw up my hands in disgust and went to play with the cat.

For entertainment, Erik, Gilbert and I frequented the nightclubs of Monmartre. I had never been to a follies and seen the singers and dancers there. Again, no one seemed at all shocked at a woman with two men, let alone that one of those men was masked. It was a rather more dissolute world that we inhabited by virtue of avoiding the Opera Quarter. Erik began an occasional indulgence in opium. I developed a fondness for absinthe, amused and intrigued by the so-called ritual that turned the strong-smelling yellow drink into a pale green treat called *louche*. I even had my own special sugar spoon after a while, shaped like the Eiffel Tower in honor of its opening. Gilbert was the only one in our trio who abstained; that way, he knew we would all get home safely.

Our lives as bored, wealthy folk came to a head after one such night at the Folies-Bergere. Erik was very high on an opium cloud; Gilbert and I were both sober. I was once again struck by the thought that this was not the life I had envisioned for myself. Things would surely be better in London. We would have a normal life, with friends and visitors.

Erik sunk into a chair and stared contemplatively into the fire Gilbert made; he would stay that way for hours. I did not think he'd written a single piece of music since the wedding mass; I would far rather his muse were upon him than this. I went up to our bedroom, silent tears flowing. All I could think of was escaping with Erik to someplace where the pain would be gone.

I had changed into a night rail when Gilbert knocked at the door. I opened it and gestured for him to enter.

"I'm concerned about Erik," he said without preamble.

"I am, too." I sat down at my vanity and began to brush out my hair. "We cannot keep living this way. I'm chafing with desire to be gone so that we can all start again."

Gilbert crossed over and took the brush from my hand. He plied it to my hair with gentle strokes, and I relaxed just as I did under Erik's ministrations. My eyes closed and my head tipped back slightly; it felt so very good.

I do not know which of us was more surprised when Gilbert

kissed me. It was a lover's kiss, albeit a tentative one.

My eyes flew open at that point, and I took back the hairbrush.

"This never happened, Gilbert. We'll not talk of it again."

"Talk of what?" My husband lounged indolently against the door frame, his cravat loose around his neck.

From the pages of Erik's journal:

I might have known it would come to this. Gilbert has moved from making calf's eyes at Claire to a kiss. Is it envy? No, it is bald-faced jealousy that I feel. He spends more time with her than I do, he fawns on her and basks in her kindness. And he is damnably handsome.

I believe Claire when she says she did not instigate the tender kiss I witnessed. All I could think of at the time was how much easier her life would be with a man who looks like Gilbert instead of a monster like me.

And yet, in his own way, Gilbert is just as broken as I, or even Claire's little Pierre. Should I be surprised that Rochambeau thrives in her kind company? I certainly have. Should I think less of another for blossoming under her hand?

Claire is right; she will not speak of it again, and neither shall I. All three of us will leave for London as soon as final arrangements are made.

For my part, I do not believe I shall touch the opium pipe again. I know now how dear a price I might pay for such a fleeting pleasure.

CHAPTER 33

August 1889

Erik kissed me, deep and passionate, while Gilbert's tongue traced a languid trail from my breast to my navel. My left hand idly toyed with Gilbert's cropped golden hair while my right caressed Erik's tumescence. Soon, one of them would fill me while I pleasured the other with my hands and mouth. Which of them would enter me first?

Two lovers, so different from one another. One fair, one dark. One with a beautiful face and twisted body, the other with a beautiful body and twisted face.

I woke with a start; the dampness at my mons told me I had climaxed in my sleep. Since that kiss from Gilbert, my dreams often ran along the same line. I was both disturbed and aroused by them.

I was, in fact, adequately disturbed by these dreams that my appetite had decreased. I could tight-lace my corsets such that Erik's long, slender fingers spanned my waist. And it was those same elegant hands that I wanted to soothe the ardorous ache in my loins provoked by those maddening, erotic dreams.

My sleeping husband was lying on his back; I slipped my night rail over my head and straddled him. With my weight on my elbows, I mouthed his throat gently and slid my aching mons along his manhood. He became more aroused as he awoke; I slid over his hardness as he became fully conscious. His hips moved in a smooth rhythm, ever deeper inside me until his climax.

"Hoyden," he whispered as I slipped off of him. He wrapped an arm around me and was soon slumbering again. I remained wakeful.

I eventually got up and dressed in a simple day gown. Antoinette had promised to pay a visit. Zareh and Erik would once again be secreted away working on emigration plans and I was wary of spending too much time alone with Gilbert. I trusted him completely, but my own dreams made me feel like an oathbreaker.

When Antoinette arrived that morning, she watched me pick at a brioche and barely sip my tea. Gilbert danced attendance on us until I sent him away. Only then did I tell my friend what had happened.

"Hmm," she said. "I see a problem, but not the one you think. Our dreams, we cannot help. The mind does what it will. You have done no wrong and broken no vow. No, my dear Claire, that is not your problem at all."

She took a deep breath.

"Your problem, Claire, is that two men live in this house, and both are in love with you."

I goggled at the very idea and began to protest.

"No, you must hear me out," Antoinette continued. "I have seen enough rival suitors in my time to know. Erik goes about his business as usual; he does not court you so much, which is common in married men." She made a face before continuing.

"But Monsieur Rochambeau has nothing but time for you. It is his job to have time for you; your husband pays him handsomely to do it. So, it is he who goes with you to the cafes, museums, gardens and market. It is he with whom you discuss books and entertainments. He is courting you in every other way, Claire. That he should steal a kiss does not surprise me.

"That Erik saw that kiss and let Gilbert live to see another day, let alone kept him on as your majordomo, is the surprise to me."

I sighed. "We are in Gilbert's debt ... and he is our friend. Like a family member."

It was the simple truth; I liked having Gilbert in the house. I was not so lonely or isolated when Erik was away.

"Then, my dear, there is only one solution. We must find someone else for Monsieur Rochambeau to love."

"You're right, of course. But where?"

"Come to the opera house this afternoon. I'm rehearsing a new corps de ballet. One of those silly girls is bound to be taken with your handsome friend."

So it was that, after many weeks of avoiding the Opera Garnier, Gilbert and I found ourselves in the plush seats. I had lost enough weight that I looked little like the slightly plump horsewoman who had once performed here; my elegant mauve day dress added another level of distance from that person. Surely, no one would ever associate the elegant Adonis sitting next to me with Francois' disheveled valet.

After the rehearsal, Antoinette invited us backstage. We were introduced vaguely as potential patrons, and I watched the young dancers flirt madly with Gilbert. He was obviously flustered at the attention; it was all rather charming to watch. To these girls, an opera patron might also mean a personal patron and a much easier life. They were somewhat relentless toward my friend; a handsome patron was particularly desirable.

Eventually, Gilbert extricated himself and we said our farewells. I remarked on the way home that the corps de ballet had been very interested in him.

"Oui, madame," Gilbert sighed. "But they are so silly and young. Not one of them is mature enough for me." When he looked at me, his dark eyes were warm with emotion.

Heaven help us all, I thought, Antoinette had been exactly right about the situation.

When we arrived back at the Place des Vosges, I found Erik waiting in the parlor. He was absolutely irate upon learning that we had gone to the Opera Garnier.

"Claire, I've ordered that we all avoid that place," he snarled.

"We were watching the ballet rehearsal at Antoinette's invitation," I replied evenly.

"I don't care. You ought to have declined."

"Is it your intention, Erik, to order every minute of Claire's life? Is such tyranny necessary?" Gilbert's temerity astonished both Erik and me.

"It is my right, whether I invoke it or no, to control my wife," Erik responded. "I am her husband, a matter I think you sometimes forget."

"Oh, for the love of all that is holy, Erik! Just stop," I shouted, and ran up the stairs to our bedroom. Heedless of my frock, I threw myself across the bed and sobbed in miserable frustration.

The comforting hand on my shoulder belonged neither to Erik nor Gilbert, but to Zareh.

"My child," he began, "How can I help?"

"You cannot," I sniffled. "Both of them are madmen."

We could hear raised voices through the floor but could not make out the words. Zareh shook his head and clicked his tongue against his teeth.

"I warned Erik that you could not live in isolation just because *he* could." He then smiled. "Madame, let us go visit your Josephine."

I threw my arms around Zareh's neck. "Nothing would make me happier. Please, just give me five minutes."

Zareh closed the door behind himself.

When I emerged downstairs, attired in my twill riding skirt and jacket, hat in hand, Erik and Gilbert were glowering at one another They stood in opposite corners of the room, angry glares flashing.

"Good day to you, Erik," Zareh said from the doorway. "I am taking Claire to see Josephine. Perhaps you will both have found your manners again by the time she returns. Come, Claire."

I followed him out the door.

CHAPTER 34

I was so happy to see Josephine. Her ears perked up at the sound of my voice and she rubbed her velvety muzzle against my cheek. Her knees were scarred, but the flesh was whole.

"How is her wind, Zareh?"

"I must tell you, Claire. My hostler says a trot now and then is the best she will ever manage. She will have a good home with me for the rest of her days. Someday, perhaps she can stay with you again, but I do not think she would travel well to England. It is cold and damp there, Claire; she would not thrive."

I nodded sadly. "I will do whatever is best for her. Please, Zareh, I want to ride her again. May I borrow a saddle?"

"But, of course." He gestured toward a groom. "Saddle Josephine for Madame LeMaitre. She is going to ride out for a while."

Once I was up on the big mare, it was as though a burden was lifted from my heart. I asked her only for a gentle walk: no tricks or *haute ecol*e. I was happy that she would be loved and cared for; she had been through so much already.

After a half hour or so, I took Josephine back into the stable and dismounted. The same young groom hurried to unsaddle her and began currying her; his hands were quick, yet gentle.

"Thank you so much for looking after her," I said. "She is very special."

"Yes, madame. This is a beautiful, good horse. I like her very much." That was obvious to me, and I felt even more relief at leaving the mare with Zareh's household.

I said my goodbyes to Josephine and Zareh dropped me off at the Place des Vosges. I had no idea what would await me when I went inside; I could only hope that my afternoon away would have allowed Erik and Gilbert to achieve a truce.

From the pages of Erik's journal:

I could conceive of only one way to explain my pain and jealousy to both Claire and Rochambeau. When she came in from her afternoon ride, I met Claire at the door wearing my Persian trousers and loose shirt, but no mask.

"Come upstairs with me, Claire," I said quietly, extending my hand to her. She took it and followed me upstairs.

I pushed open our bedroom door; Gilbert was seated on Claire's vanity chair, just as I had instructed him. His eyes were wide with confusion.

"Please, Claire, I would like you to undress now." I kept my tone as calm as possible.

"Erik, I cannot ..." she protested.

"Just do it. Gilbert has seen you in your night rail; surely the sight of your corset and stockings will not prove his undoing."

With an air of puzzlement, she did as I asked. I noticed how tightly her corset was laced; she had not been eating much of late and was slimming to a fetishist's dream. I preferred her more rounded silhouette, but so be it.

"To your vanity, please, my dear. Gilbert is going to unpin and brush out your hair. I know how you like that." I could not keep the hint of sadness from my voice.

When Claire's locks were hanging smoothly down her back, almost reaching her tightly cinched waist, I looked Gilbert in the eye.

"A beautiful picture, is she not? Now, you may watch and see what my life has been like. Treated like a eunuch in Persia, and watching from afar as other men kissed the woman I love."

Claire stood silent in the middle of the room. I took her in my arms and bent down to kiss her. I felt so melancholy and cruel as her lips met mine. She began to sob in my arms and I held her, crooning gently. At last, I looked up at Gilbert; his eyes were downcast.

"You now stand where I have stood, mon ami. You know what it is to have someone you love out of your reach, and to know you have overstepped your bounds in trying to change things. And now, let us truly not talk of this again. We have a move to plan."

"I will stay behind," Gilbert whispered.

I realized that he at last truly comprehended my position concerning his infatuation with Claire, and assured him it was not necessary.

"We will need you there, Gilbert."

When Erik walked out of the room, Gilbert followed him. I had never felt so used, and yet so guilty at the same time. I had done nothing wrong, but Erik's behavior had been just as cruel to me as it had been to Gilbert. How dare he humiliate me so!

I began to pin my hair back into place, annoyed that it had been used as part of a punishment. I finished dressing quickly and strode out of the house, hat in hand. This would not happen again.

It was early evening and the shop at Les Halles where I might have accomplished my mission was closed. Instead, I went to the opera house and sought out Antoinette. I told her what had happened and what I wanted. She, in turn, simply shook her head and took me to the wigmaker.

CHAPTER 35

From the pages of Erik's journal:

I do not know what possessed me to humiliate Claire and Gilbert that way. Gilbert repaired to his room and Claire dressed and left the house. It was nearly two hours before she let herself back in, wearing a cloak that I recognized as one of Antoinette's. It was a fancy cloak, with wiring to hold the hood away from a lady's evening coiffure.

"Claire, my love, where have you been? I have been so worried."

She removed the cloak then, and I was astonished at what I saw. Her chestnut brown locks had been cut to shoulder length, and arranged in a tousle of curls by someone very skilled with hot tongs and hairpins. She opened her reticule and held out five francs to me.

"The wigmaker at the opera house gave me this in exchange for your possession." Her tone was icy and, when I did not take the coins, she dropped them at my feet. "I would not want my hair to be the cause of any further conflict."

She turned away from me and headed for the stairs; Gilbert came out of his room upon hearing her voice and took in her altered appearance as she sailed past him, leaving both of us gaping in her wake.

Dear god, I thought as I looked at my reflection in the mirror, what have I done? It had been the wigmaker's idea to curl my hair after he cut off my long braid and paid me for it. Several more snips here and there to shape and even the length. Hot tongs and pearl-topped hairpins to hold the curls in position. Even my brows had been reshaped; I did not look like myself at all.

I added a touch of color to my mouth and kohl around my eyes. If they wanted to treat me like a trifling whore between themselves, at least I would look the part.

I stripped down to corset and stockings again and was rifling my wardrobe for a dinner dress when Erik entered the room and closed the door behind himself. He was still unmasked, his shirt open at the collar, and his eyes dark with desire as they raked over me.

"My god, Claire," he said quietly under my defiant gaze. "Do you have any idea how you look?"

"Rather like an unfashionable strumpet just at the moment, I should think."

"Oh, no, my dear," he responded. "You have no idea." He unbuttoned his shirt the rest of the way. "No, my dear ... you look like a creature from Faerie. Your nape begs to be kissed, and those curls cry out to be caressed by a lover's fingers."

He crossed the room, and soon his actions matched his words. Despite myself, I shivered with desire as his sinful mouth caressed my neck and shoulders. He led me over to the bed and sat me on the edge."

"Lie back, vixen," he whispered, and knelt between my thighs. He ran his fingers through the curls at my mons. "You have behaved rather badly today, I am afraid. But then, so have I. Permit me to make it up to you."

Then he set his mouth to me. Every stroke of his hot tongue on my flesh was agony and ecstasy at the same time. Each sensation was magnified beyond anything I had ever experienced; my ire had inflamed me more than I had thought possible.

When I climaxed, I was amazed at the strength of the waves that came over me. I had not even removed corset and stockings, and Erik had not entered me. Still, I was shaken by the depth of my pleasure. I caressed Erik's hair.

"If you thought to make yourself unattractive to me, Claire," he said raggedly, joining me on the bed, "you have failed miserably. It is not your hair; it is you."

He opened his trousers and slid deep inside me. He held my hands pinned over my head and nipped at my earlobes and throat while he pounded deep into my sex. His own climax was hard and explosive as he tensed within me.

"And now, hoyden, you should dress for dinner." He slid out of me, trailing his fingers across my climax-drenched mons and sensually licking just the tips. "We will continue with this later tonight."

CHAPTER 36

London, England
September 1889

In hindsight, it was amazing how quickly the weeks passed from that time until we moved into our fashionable London home. Pierre, now sleek and plump, was generally found entwining himself around my ankles as I set the new house to rights. Zareh managed to remove some of Erik's furnishings from below the Opera House and moved them into the townhouse for us. My favorite piece was the beautifully carved bed with its motif of nymphs and satyrs, now upstairs in the master suite. Yet again, our life was one of potential scandal; Erik and I did not keep separate boudoirs in the English fashion.

I had a hard time accustoming myself to having a staff. There was our driver, Michael Stubbins, with a handsome horse he called Blackjack. Michael's smiling wife Maggie was our cook. Their daughter, 10-year-old Dolly, was learning from her mother and functioned as our downstairs maid. Their 15-year-old son, Jamie, was learning under Michael's tutelage to be an hostler. Gilbert continued as Erik's valet and our majordomo. I initially refused a maid of my own, as I had enough of a challenge asking others to do for me what I'd always done for myself. However, Erik insisted and so it was that I met Maggie's sister Honor. I was grateful when I saw a light in Gilbert's eyes upon meeting Honor for the first time; the quiet, red-haired girl clearly approved of him, for she returned his smile and watched him make his way up the stairs.

We had barely settled in to the house when neighbors began calling, leaving visiting cards in a salver on the foyer sideboard. I dreaded the afternoons when I was "at home" to guests. Our first caller was Lady Alice Harrington, who lived two houses away; she had iron-colored hair, a jaw to match, and a bosom like the prow of a ship. She left a calling card, and invited us to a musical evening at their home just a few nights hence. Lady Harrington informed us that her daughter, Olympia, would be performing several songs and asked that we prepare something ourselves, should we be so inclined, to share with the gathering.

I purchased my own visiting cards, which proved to be something of an ordeal. At the stationery counter at Selfridges Department Store, I ordered my two sets, plain ivory stock with "Madame Erik LeMaitre" on the front and an address on the back of one set. The other set was blank on the reverse; those were for people to whom I did not wish to be at home. I thought the custom unspeakably impolite, but was told by the shop girl that this was what was done. She also explained, in an exasperated tone, that I could only have my own name, Claire, on the card if I were widowed.

As I walked away after paying for my purchase and arranging for its delivery, I could not help overhearing the girl's remark about "that bloody ignorant French woman."

Before long the musical evening was upon us. I was quite excited about the event and Honor prepared my toilette with care. I wore a wine-colored gown with jet beaded trim; dark ruby jewels accented my throat and hair. Erik was his usual elegant self in evening attire and kid leather mask.

In The Eye of The Beholder

I never told Alice why Erik wore the mask. She had once made a presumptuous remark about "an injury in the Crimea, I suppose," and I did nothing to dissuade her from the notion. Erik would have been a very young boy at the time of the Crimean war, but it did not matter to me what the woman believed. As we went through the reception line, I surmised that her other guests had been told the same tale, as few of them looked twice at the mask. Erik was as charming as an ambassador during the light supper we enjoyed before going into the music room.

The first performance of the evening was by the Honorable Miss Olympia. She sang Joseph Strauss's "Laughing Song" passably enough, but Erik cringed during some of the obligatos. His finely tuned ear made him a harsh critic, but he applauded politely with the rest. Many other guests also contributed, playing piano or violin.

At length, Alice turned to me. "Well, Claire, will you or your husband perform for us this evening?"

"I would be honored, Madame Harrington," Erik replied, "to play and sing a piece of my own composition."

With that, he made his way to the piano and seated himself at the bench. He played an introductory phrase and then performed the English translation of a song that he had once sung to me in the townhouse: that same song of surrender in the darkness that had captured my soul. There was not even a murmur amongst those present as they listened to his beautiful tenor and watched his hands move across the keys. Olympia Harrington barely breathed and I noticed that she couldn't take her eyes from his face. I also noted that many of the matrons were employing their fans with tremendous vigor.

God in heaven, I thought, Olympia's going to develop a *tendresse* for him -- and some of the mamas are not far behind.

When the last phrase of the song echoed away, there was a brief silence and then a huge burst of applause and "bravos."

"You really should have told me," Alice whispered. "I had no idea your husband was a composer and singer."

"We met at the Opera Garnier," I revealed.

"He's brilliant," she rejoined.

"He's beautiful," I heard Olympia remark to her mother.

"And married," her mother rejoined. "Set your cap elsewhere, daughter."

The shine in Olympia's eyes promised disobedience.

CHAPTER 37

Shortly after Erik's performance, the Harringtons' guests began to say their farewells. We waited in the foyer until Michael brought the carriage around. Mrs. Harrington and her daughter chose that moment to descend upon me.

"Mrs. LeMaitre," Alice began, "My Olympia is entertaining the notion that your husband should become her singing instructor. I will brook no resistance in this matter, of course. What Olympia wants, she gets."

"Really, Madame Harrington," I responded, "I could not say for certain whether Erik is interested in taking on a student at this time. We are only newly come to London and are still putting our household in order."

"Perhaps you didn't hear Mama," Olympia interrupted. "I want your husband to be my instructor."

"And perhaps you did not hear me, my dear," I responded with a smile that did not quite reach my eyes. "My husband may not wish to take on any students at this time, and I will not speak for him."

Fortunately, Erik came to my rescue by announcing that our coach was ready. With an indignant cough, Lady Harrington announced that she would leave a card on me to call at my earliest convenience to one of her at-home afternoons.

Once we were in the carriage, I related my exchange with the Harringtons to Erik. He dismissed my concerns with a laugh.

"My dear, that child will never tread the boards at Covent Garden. I have no intention of taking her on as a student. Just forget about her. As for the mother, go to her at-home and charm her friends senseless."

We arrived home long after the other members of the household had retired to their quarters, and Erik sent Michael home with his thanks. He let me into our townhouse and helped me off with my wrap, setting his lips gently to the nape of my neck.

"Madame LeMaitre," he whispered, his breath warm on my skin, "Shall we away to our scandalously shared boudoir?"

My shuddering intake of breath at even his gentlest touch cried my assent. Erik picked me up easily and carried me upstairs. I wrapped my arms around his neck, running my fingers through his sable locks, and kissed him deeply. I was still astonished at my body's response to the man whom I had married, and I reveled in every moment of it. His lovemaking became more masterful by the day, and I reveled in that as well.

Erik established an office in the City of London proper, and went there each day to manage his accounts and business interests. He rose early and usually departed before I was fully awake. I was not yet accustomed to my leisurely life, despite those dissolute days toward the end of our stay in Paris, and chafed at the inactivity of a proper society lady's days.

I rang for Honor to attend me. I intended to spend the day with Maggie in the kitchen, teaching her some of my favorite recipes; I found English cuisine entirely too bland for my taste.

Honor laced my corset up the back and I donned the dark green wool skirt made from the remains of the frock Giraud had torn the day he tried to attack me. My blouse was a fine silk Garibaldi, with pintucks on the bodice.

I sent Honor on ahead of me to the kitchen and played with Pierre for a while. The sleek little cat wore a red ribbon around his neck and I spoiled him dreadfully. He loved to snuggle and purr, and at the same time remained a playful creature who made me smile. He bounded down the stairs ahead of me, stopping to rub at my ankles as I followed.

We had barely gotten settled in the kitchen to discuss menus when the door knocker could be heard. Dolly answered the door and explained to the visitor that "Madame is not at home to callers today."

"She'll be at home to me." Lady Harrington's tone was stentorian as she pushed past Dolly. "Now, where is your mistress?"

I left the kitchen and faced Alice. I really did not wish for company.

"I do believe Dolly informed you that I am not at home to visitors."

"You're plainly at home," the woman said stubbornly, "and you will hear me out. My daughter has it in her head to become an opera singer. She also has it in her head that no instructor will do but your husband. For reasons I fail to understand, she is determined to sing at Covent Garden. As my husband and I are patrons of that opera, I am certain that she will do so."

The woman's arrogance astonished me, but I gestured for her to continue.

"We will pay handsomely, of course."

"Madame Harrington," I interrupted. "Does our household appear to be in need of funds?"

"That is hardly the point, Mrs. LeMaitre," she responded. "The point is that Olympia is our only child, and she will have whatever she wants."

"Ah. She will have whatever she wants," I responded evenly, "regardless of the convenience of the other parties in question?"

"You were clearly brought up poorly," was the next sally. "A true lady would never dream of questioning her betters."

"And who are Madame's betters?" Gilbert inquired from the stairs. He was an arrestingly handsome picture as he came down the stairs in a bespoke suit of dark brown superfine and gold brocade waistcoat.

"Would those betters be the parties who do not understand etiquette? You have twice been informed that Madame is not at home to visitors. You will depart, or I shall send for both the master and the gendarmerie ... the police." Gilbert continued to descend the stairwell and his last remark was addressed eye to eye with Alice.

Astonished into silence, she made her way back to the door, making a great show of dropping her card in the hallway salver. Clearly she had not expected my majordomo to be so forceful.

"Don't bother to show me out," she huffed, and slammed the door behind her.

With a sigh, I went back to the kitchen and returned my attention to the cookery books that Maggie and I were using to select our menus. Yet, the interruptions continued.

Erik came home for the day at noon time and we had just sat down to luncheon when Olympia Harrington, unchaperoned, pulled her high-wheeled phaeton into the stable yard. Michael ran to greet her. The poor pony was breathing heavily, having both gag bit and bearing reins added to her harness for "style's sake" and being unable to use either lung or muscle to best advantage.

Olympia alighted, dropping the reins with a haughty gesture that presumed, correctly in this case, that someone would see to her horse. As Michael undid the bearing rein so that the horse could drink some water, the blonde girl approached the house and, as her mother had earlier, pushed her way past Dolly.

"Mrs. LeMaitre, Mother told me you were at home today, but perhaps she is wrong. Surely you do not receive while dressed as a shop girl." She smugly smoothed her elegant silk walking suit. "And, Monsieur LeMaitre, how wonderful to find you at home, too." She extended her hand, and Erik sketched a bow over it.

"Madame LeMaitre is not at home to visitors," Erik murmured. "I'm afraid your mother was mistaken."

"Oh, no. She was here earlier. She even left a card."

"Erik, my dear," I said quietly, laying my hand on his arm. "I will explain after Miss Harrington has departed. Really, my dear," I added, turning to the girl, "Your mother was informed that I was not at home to guests, and I cannot imagine why she would tell you otherwise."

"Really. Well, then, I will complete my business and be on my way."

"Yes, please," Erik intoned.

"Oh, very well," she said as she stomped petulantly back toward the door. "Mother has asked that you join us in our box at Covent Garden for the opera on Christmas Eve. It's a mixed program, and one of the singers is from France. She thought that you might enjoy it." She dropped the written invitation and two billets on the hallway salver.

"You may tell your mother that we are honored to join you," Erik replied. "Would you like to wait for a written response to take to her?"

"No, that won't be necessary."

With that, the girl flounced toward her gig, refused Michael's offer of assistance to step up, and flicked her buggy whip across the little mare's back. I noted with some glee that the pony's bearing rein was gone from the harness and wondered when Olympia would notice.

"Nasty things, these," Michael said as he produced the strap from a pocket. "Young madame won't pay any mind, but the mare will be the happier for it." His smile was grim as he touched his cap and returned to the stable.

"I think, my dear," Erik said as he closed the door, "that you had best tell me about Madame Harrington's visit this morning."

CHAPTER 38

October-November 1889

Alice Harrington invited me to several of her at-homes. Such visits were the main activity for ladies of her station: tea parties with gossip, at a different woman's house each day of the week. I found them dreary affairs; listening to the scandals of Lady Thus-and-So grew dull with repetition.

Eventually, I tried holding my own afternoon salons. I worked with Maggie to recreate some of my favorite recipes for madeleines and cheese crisps, and had Russian tea and American coffee on offer. The ladies came to the first one in droves, and I was so very excited. They were chatting away, eating the treats and sipping their hot drinks. At last, I thought, perhaps I have found a way to fit in.

It was only when I stepped out for a moment to get another tray of madeleines rather than ringing for them, that I learned the truth. I was returning with the plate when I overheard Alice Harrington discussing me.

"Well, she is French, you know. They're all lazy creatures. Her husband is a charming man; pity about the mask. Wounded in the Crimea as a young man, you know. My daughter is quite taken with his singing and wants to have lessons of him, but the wife won't hear of it. They've no children; she's barren, I'm sure of it. My Olympia would be happy to marry him if he'd put the wife aside."

"Well, Alice," said another lady in response, "I think she's no better than she should be. Look at these books she reads: Balzac and Hugo. I ask you. Everyone knows French books are filled with filth. And I hear she drinks absinthe."

All of the ladies made shocked sounds at that.

I stepped back into the room, pretending to have heard nothing. "Here are some more madeleines, my friends. Please, help yourselves."

When they left, I was surprised to see a pile of visiting cards on the hallway salver. Perhaps it had gone better than I had thought.

Not one of them had an address on the back. Not one of the ladies whom I had entertained was at home to me.

It became harder and harder for me to get up in the mornings; some days, I chose to simply stay abed and sleep. Pierre would curl up with me and we would nap the day away. I had no appetite at all: Honor had to take in the waist of my skirts. It didn't matter, really, because all I wanted to wear was the lavender flannel night rail Erik had bought for me during our brief honeymoon. Maggie tried to entice me to eat something, preparing nourishing soups that would be easy to digest, but to no avail. I would drink some water and nibble at bread, but that was as far as it went.

Erik had a doctor visit, but he could find nothing wrong with me. Erik told me later that the doctor also advised him to get a child on me as soon as possible, because I was obviously melancholy due to barrenness. Erik knew I did not particularly want children and, when he told the doctor that, the doctor advised him to kill Pierre.

"Take away her cat and she'll want a child to dote on instead," he'd said. "All women want children, but some of them just don't know it yet."

Erik escorted the doctor to the door himself at that point, telling him that if his advice was to kill something I loved then his advice was not needed in our household.

Thereafter, I often stayed abed. Erik gave orders that I was not to be left alone. When he was at his office, Honor or Gilbert would stay in the room with me. Honor did needlework most of the time and did not speak to me. Gilbert told me that she felt it inappropriate to discuss things with her employers, that she believed in what she called "keeping to her place."

Some days, I would pretend to be asleep, listening to the two of them talk when they relieved each other. That Honor and Gilbert cared for one another was apparent, despite her blunt attitude that he needed to learn "more English ways." She even pronounced his name in the English fashion, making it sound harsh and hard to my ear. I was nevertheless pleased that my dear friend had found female companionship, regardless of her plainspoken ways.

Gilbert developed an interest in art and took up drawing. I would sometimes wake to find him sketching something, but he would never show the drawings to me. He claimed that they were unschooled and that he would show me his work someday, but not just now.

One morning, Gilbert brought me a gift: a soft stuffed horse covered with velvety black plush.

"It's Josephine," he whispered as he settled the toy in my arms.

I wrapped my arms around the soft pony and fell asleep, awakening after luncheon when Erik came in to check on me. He was bemused by Gilbert's choice of a gift, and said so. But I was pleased by the gesture. I missed France, Josephine, and our life in Paris more than words could say; Gilbert's present was a reminder of happy times.

Some days, Gilbert would persuade me to go on an outing with him; the British Museum was a particular favorite. On those occasions, I could forget my troubles and pretend that we were still back in Paris. Gilbert would take his sketch pad and draw the sculptures, or make quick studies of the other patrons. Those excursions were the high points of my existence, and yet there were far more times when I could not arouse myself enough to leave the house.

After nearly a month of me staying abed, Erik had another idea. When we awoke that morning, he announced his intention to seek out a riding horse for me. I sat up in bed at that; the idea of riding again instead of being driven everywhere sent a surge of happiness through my entire body.

"Do you want me to go with you?" I inquired as I watched him put the final touches to his attire. Riding breeches, a tweed coat and a crisply pressed shirt and neckstock presented a picture of country elegance.

"No, I'll take Michael along. You remain abed as long as you wish." He leaned down to kiss me gently.

As I was now wide awake, however, I got out of bed and donned a wrapper. I made my way downstairs to the kitchen, where Maggie and Dolly were already at work.

"Please, might I have a cup of tea and some toast?" I sank into a chair; the lack of activity had left me rather weak.

Gilbert came in the back entrance with more wood for the stove and began to fuss about me immediately. "Claire, er, Madame ... are you comfortable? Can I get you anything?"

"No, mon vieux, I am fine. Erik is going to get me a horse today.

I need to have something to eat if I am to start riding again. I cannot be a slug-a-bed."

Maggie and Gilbert exchanged a look at that point. They understood, far better than I did, that I had not been in bed out of sheer laziness, but that I was still in a state of melancholia that only time would eradicate.

"Well, Ma'am Claire," Maggie said as she set the tea and toast in front of me. "You eat that slow-like. Let us know what else you need."

What an interesting world I live in, I thought as I sipped the tea. My so-called servants are more kind than my so-called friends.

After I had broken my fast, I asked Gilbert to help me up the stairs and to ring for Honor to attend me. I wanted a bath first and foremost, and washed both body and hair twice before I felt clean enough. Honor laced my corset as tight as it would go and still it was loose on me; I had lost entirely too much weight and she clucked sadly.

"We'll have to get you to the corset-maker soon, Ma'am Claire. This French one is just too big now." She made a pretty moue.

It was my favorite China-blue silk; I hoped that a competent corsettier could take it in. Over my plainest petticoat went a dark blue skirt; my blouse was a lighter blue. My hair was just past my shoulders; a dark blue ribbon band kept it out of my eyes.

Gilbert helped me down the stairs. I could not help noticing, once again, the smile in his eyes when he looked at my pretty, red-haired maid.

"Gilbert, my friend, are you courting?" I asked as he helped me to the parlor and settled me onto the chaise longue near the fire.

My handsome friend blushed red. "Yes, Claire. Honor and I are courting. She is a good woman."

"Then I wish you the best of fortune."

I was prevented from saying anything further at the moment by Jamie bursting into the parlor.

"Papa's just bringing the carriage 'round. They must have the horses!" he exclaimed.

"Well, Gilbert, if you would be so kind as to help me outside to see what Erik has brought home, I would be much obliged."

When I got out to the yard, Michael was just untying a mettlesome bay gelding from the back of the carriage.

"Where is Monsieur LeMaitre?" I inquired.

"He's coming along with the horse car," Michael replied, an odd look on his face. "This beautiful horse he picked out for himself, but I don't know about the one he said you'd want." He shook his head slowly. "I just don't know."

I occupied myself with rubbing the gelding's velvety nose and speaking quietly to him in French while Michael brushed him down. Before long, the horse car came into view. Erik alighted from the rear and paid the driver ... and then led out the saddest, thinnest chestnut mare I had ever seen.

"You see, ma'am," Michael said. "That's the horse he said you'd want."

Erik led the poor horse over to a stall. Her gait was halting, for her feet were overgrown, and her ribs were so visible that she might have been an anatomy lesson. Nevertheless, I could see that her breeding was good; her face had the slightly convex profile that betrayed Arab blood, and her conformation overall was excellent.

"Better that one should go to the knacker," Jamie muttered.

"Ah, no, Master James," Erik responded. "You see, Claire has a way of loving broken creatures back to life. This horse is more than she appears to be. Look at her teeth."

"I'm not touching that sack of bones," the boy responded.

"You'll do as the master says," Michael responded, but still his son stayed put.

"Very well, then," I said. I lifted the poor mare's muzzle gently and put my thumbs into the bars of her mouth. She opened obediently, revealing teeth that showed her to be less than 10 years old.

"Erik, she's young yet!" I explained.

"That she is. I paid five pounds for her, since that's what the drayer said the knacker would give him." He smiled sadly. "Do you think you could work with her?"

"I can try," I said, for my heart had gone out to the poor animal who had come down in the world and known a very hard life. "First thing, Michael, please trim her feet. And Jamie, you help me brush her. I suspect we'll find that she's beautiful one day; we just cannot see it yet."

"What are you going to call her?" Erik asked.

"I don't know," I responded, working my fingers through a tangle in her dull red mane. "Pauvre ange." I reverted to my native language for just a moment, calling the horse "poor angel," and there I found my inspiration.

"Erik, I think I shall call her Angel."

Erik continued stroking the poor horse and talking to her quietly, his hypnotic voice as effective on her as a sedative. She lifted her feet willingly for Michael to cut away the overgrown hooves and pull off the shoes that should have been changed weeks ago. She leaned into the curry comb and dry, dull hair shed onto the cobblestones as I worked on one side and Jamie the other.

"You'll not be able to ride her for a while," Michael cautioned. "I'll need to find you a sidesaddle."

Erik laughed aloud at that. "Michael, my lady wife will scandalize you and the entire neighborhood. She rides beautifully ... and astride."

Jamie blushed beet-red at the thought and plied his brushes with a bit more vigor.

I handed my curry comb to Jamie to put away with the rest of the grooming tools and slipped my hand through the cheekpiece of poor Angel's head collar. She looked better already with the dry, dead hair combed away; she was a beautiful red tone underneath. Unfortunately, my ministrations to the horse had resulted in my blue skirt being covered with red hair; Honor would be very frustrated when it came time to brush it.

If the truth be told, Angel and I healed one another in many ways. I grew physically stronger as I worked with her each day. The first day I had Jamie give me a leg up to lay across her back, my heart began to sing as it had not in many months. I loved riding, and even a sedate walk around the yard improved my state of mind. I was still melancholic at times; I had given up on the salon and no longer went to anyone's at-home days; I did not fit in that way and realized that I did not want to. If people looked askance that my servants were my friends, why, let them do so. I would rather be among those who cared.

CHAPTER 39

December 1889

One day when I felt up to activity, it snowed in London. I had planned to visit a museum, but Gilbert had a different idea.

"There is a frozen pond at the Tower, Claire. Perhaps you would like to try ice skating? I would be happy to accompany you. Alas," he gestured toward his leg, "I shan't be joining you on the ice. Nevertheless, I could take you there and back while Erik is at the office."

"It's the Stubbins' day off, Gilbert. If we take the carriage, one of us shall have to stay with the horse. That wouldn't be much company for either of us. I might just as well to stay home in that event."

"Then we shall have the grand adventure of taking the omnibus."

Gilbert would brook no resistance, and I was glad to have something to do. I had never tried ice skating, but was grateful to Gilbert for his willingness to help me. The days that I felt like trying to do anything were crucial, and could not be ignored. So, I dressed warmly in a grey tweed walking suit and black boots. Over the top went a bottle green coat with black fur trim, matching bonnet and muff. We took the omnibus to the Tower and I rented a pair of skates to attach to my boots.

I was frightened at first and a little off-balance. I fell more than once, but with the assistance of some children eventually learned the correct motions to propel myself around the pond. There were many folk out on the ice, laughing and enjoying themselves, and I could not help but feel my mood lighten.

After I returned my skates, my legs rubbery with exertion, Gilbert bought mugs of tea and roasted chestnuts from a nearby vendor. We watched the other skaters for a while, sharing our snack in companionable silence. When we finished our treat, I thanked Gilbert.

"It is nothing, Claire. Seeing a bit of color back in your cheeks and a smile on your face are worth more than gold to me." Gilbert's gaze was penetrating at first, and then he looked away. "I should take you home soon, Claire."

"Perhaps you could help me with my Christmas shopping before we go," I suggested. I was not ready to be shut up in the house again today. Tomorrow might be different; I had to take advantage of my improved mood.

So, we again took an omnibus into Knightsbridge to shop at Harrods. We browsed the entire seven floors. In the mens' furnishings department, Gilbert especially admired a walking stick with a faceted blue glass knob for a handle.

"That's a gentleman's stick for certain," he said. "It's very handsome." He examined the price tag and put the stick back in the display.

"Let's see what we can find for the family," he said.

"What are you planning to buy for Honor?" I asked.

"I don't really know, Claire. She is a hard one to read. She doesn't appear to care for frills and things; she's said more than once that she's a simple girl and not 'one o' them toffs' she could name. I think she may be something of a snob."

"I think she may just be sounding you out, Gilbert. She's a good girl and you could do much worse for yourself."

"I suppose you are right," Gilbert smiled. "She is a very appropriate match for someone like me."

"She is quite pretty, too," I smiled.

"She is that. I am a rather lucky fellow." His smile broadened, and I could not help grinning back at him in delight.

I was grateful for Gilbert's help with the packages at the end of the trip, for there were gifts for the Stubbins family and Erik to manage. We hailed a hansom cab to take us home with our bounty. I would shop for Gilbert on another occasion, that I might surprise him with that walking stick. I owed so much to him, and he would be pleased.

From the pages of Erik's journal:

I have been so worried about Claire these past months that I have neglected my journals. Fortunately, I listened to myself instead of the doctor: obviously what Claire wanted was not an infant but another horse. The physical change in her has been remarkable. She has more of an appetite than before, but sometimes I think she is eating only so that she can work with Angel and not because she tastes the food. She is not the happy woman I married; I attribute that to the damp, dark weather here more than anything else. She has welcomed me in her bed each night, although her ardor is not what it has been in the past. Again, I believe this is part of her melancholia. I am confident that she still loves me. Still, these months have not been easy.

I must write about the Christmas program we attended with the Harringtons. Claire was attired in the beautiful blue gown and jewels I gave her in Paris and fit in with the society matrons as though she were to the manor born. For my part, keeping company in large crowds still wore on me, and I had no idea then what was in store on that evening.

We sat through several vignettes and arias, until there was only one piece left before the intermission. It was at that point that Olympia Harrington turned to me with a sly smile.

"Monsieur LeMaitre, I wonder whether this singer might be known to you. The Vicomtesse de Chagny -- Christine -- says she sang at the Opera Garnier during the same time that you were there."

I felt the color drain from my face, and when I turned to Claire I saw a mixture of emotions in her eyes that I could not even describe. One of them was certainly fear, but of what I could not say.

"I ... do not believe I knew a Vicomtesse de Chagny," I muttered, hoping the half-truth would suffice. I cursed myself for not looking at the programs we had been handed, for then I would have known and could have planned some kind of stratagem to depart before there was a chance that Christine and I would run into each other.

"I've taken the liberty of inviting Madame de Chagny to join us here during the intermission," Olympia was saying. "I thought it might be amusing if the two of you had an opportunity to reminisce about a place where you both sang, whether or not you knew one another."

Claire blanched: we were well and truly trapped.

How we both sat through Christine's breathtakingly beautiful performance of Delibes' "Flower Song" from *Lakme* was a puzzle. I am ashamed to admit that I could not take my eyes from Christine's face; it was more rounded than when I had last seen her, and it took me a moment to understand why. She was, as we said in France, *enceinte* -- with child. For a brief moment, I hated Raoul de Chagny, the father-to-be, with all of my heart.

After the piece ended and Christine had taken her curtsies, I prayed for Claire to have a clever reason for us to leave. However, her keen wits failed us both, and before we knew it Christine was entering the box. Fortunately, my back was to her so that she did not immediately recognize me.

"Madame de Chagny," Olympia was saying, "here is the gentleman I told you about who was at our musical evening and sang so beautifully. He has sung in the Opera Garnier; that is where he met his wife, who is also here. Monsieur and Madame LeMaitre, I should like to introduce Madame Christine de Chagny."

At that point, I had little choice but to stand and bow over Christine's hand. She started visibly when she recognized me, and Olympia's quick eyes could not help but notice.

"You know one another, then?" she asked.

"Erik, that is Monsieur LeMaitre, and I are slightly acquainted through professional circumstances. I have not, however, had the honor of meeting Madame LeMaitre," Christine managed. What a cool liar she was, a side of her I had never seen until now. Professional circumstances, indeed.

Claire curtsied and made her greeting to Christine.

"Madame la Vicomtesse, I am honored to meet you. Erik has remarked on what a gifted singer you were."

My wife placed a slight emphasis on the last word and I saw, not for the first time, that the cat I married had claws. It was then that I identified what I'd seen on her face: not just fear, but desperate jealousy borne of the idea that I might still love the double-timing minx who stood there in front of me as though butter wouldn't melt in her mouth.

Up until that very moment, I had thought the same thing. Both of us were wrong.

As I would learn later, I was the only one who realized that I no longer loved Christine.

Claire continued to make polite conversation for a few minutes and then excused herself from the box. I could vaguely hear her speaking to the box attendant, reverting to her native French.

"J'ai besoin de cracher," she said to the woman ... I need to vomit. She then remembered herself. "I am unwell. Could you send an usher to find a doctor for me?"

While all of this was going on, I sought to extricate myself from the less-than-desirable company of Madame de Chagny and the Harrington family. When I finally found a break in the conversation that would allow me to exit, I too sought the attendant.

"Sir," she said, "the lady looked awfully pale and was ill. I found a doctor, sir, Doctor Treves. He's seeing to the lady in the lounge."

"Take me to her. I need to be there with her." I raked my hand through my hair, for a change heedless of my appearance. "I'll call for my carriage."

The usher took me to the lounge, where Claire lay on a chaise longue. I introduced myself to the physician, a Doctor Sir Frederick

Treves.

"She's resting, sir. She's been ill at her stomach. I'm a surgeon, but I don't think she needs operating. I think she needs observation. I can arrange to admit her to the hospital, or to see her at home."

"What's wrong with her?"

"I don't know yet, my friend."

"I don't want to be apart from her when she's unwell. She ..." I sat down in a chair and dropped my face into my hands. "She loves me regardless, and I need to be with her. I'll take her home."

"What on earth do you mean by that, sir? 'She loves me regardless' is a strong statement."

With that, I reached behind my head and undid the mask, revealing my face to the doctor. His eyes widened with interest as I tied the mask back in place.

"She loves me in spite of this hideous face. I would die for her, and every pain that she feels is my own."

"I'll call on her tomorrow at your home if you'll give me an address. For now, she really must be kept quiet."

I called for my carriage and delivered Claire to our home. Then, reverting to a pattern I had long thought behind me, I had Michael take me to the Chinatown at Limehouse, where I sought out the arms of Morpheus in an opium den.

CHAPTER 40

I awoke slightly disoriented, but in my own bed. I remembered falling ill at the opera gala and that Erik had brought me home. I had never felt physically ill from emotion before, but there it was. I was sick at my stomach with jealousy over how Erik still felt about Madame Christine de Chagny. There was no way to mistake what I saw in his eyes.

I got out of bed and paced the floor, my mood dark and brooding. I was tired of feeling useless; the dignified and proper life of a society matron with servants and a fine townhouse was not what I craved. I wanted to work with poor Angel, nursing her back to health and riding her through the streets. I wanted to sing at the top of my voice if I so chose, something that would have gone completely unnoticed back at the opera house.

Most of all, I wished I had never laid eyes on Madame de Chagny. Then, I could have gone on naively believing that I was first in my husband's heart instead of my certain knowledge that I was only second best to him.

A tap on my door, and my reply, admitted Maggie to my room. She brought me a tray with tea and toast and asked how I was doing. I shook my head sadly and nibbled at the food with little appetite. Gilbert followed close on her heels and closed the door behind Maggie so that we were alone.

I bared my soul to Gilbert, just as I had done so many times in France. I knew he would understand. However, when I reached the part in my frustrated narrative about being second best, he stopped me.

"Is that truly what you think? That Erik thinks you are second-best, and that you are useless?"

I nodded my assent. I could not imagine going through a life fussing over dinner menus and whether or not the lappets on my lace breakfast cap had the right amount of starch.

"You matter to more people than you will ever know, Claire." He took my hand in his and gently brushed the knuckles with his lips. "I'll leave you to your rest. And I will also try to find where Erik has gone."

It had not even occurred to me that Erik was not home. I sighed with frustration.

Maggie knocked on the door again and admitted Doctor Treves.

"How are you doing, madame? Recovered somewhat?" He looked somewhat askance at Gilbert, whom I then introduced as our majordomo and explained that he was looking after me in my husband's absence.

"Your husband is an interesting case, Madame LeMaitre," Dr. Treves replied. "I think I know what your problem is. You need useful activity, and I have just the answer. Dress yourself and meet me downstairs; I will wait for you."

Gilbert and the doctor took their leave. With Maggie's help, I dressed in a starched shirtwaist and woolen skirt, threw a shawl over the lot and pinned on my serviceable brown bonnet. I met the doctor downstairs, prepared for whatever he had in store for me.

From the pages of Erik's journal:

After returning from my night of debauchery, I went out to the stable. I wanted to be with Angel, and it took me a few moments to understand why. Both of us were broken creatures whom Claire loved despite our deformities and our past.

It was there that Gilbert found me. He tried to convey to me what Claire was feeling: that the life I so desperately wanted to give her was not what she wanted. I truly believed that if I could bless her with material wealth, she would know how much she meant to me, and yet it appeared that I was wrong. I was at a loss as to what might be the appropriate thing to do. I said as much to Gilbert, who just clucked his tongue and left me alone after telling me that Claire had accompanied Dr. Treves to the hospital.

I took off my jacket and mask, then my waistcoat and tie, and rolled up my sleeves. I picked up a soft grooming brush and stroked it across Angel's red coat. Her eyes rolled, and I spoke quietly to calm her. Even with the work that Claire had done thusfar, the poor horse was still frightened of humans and did not yet trust that she would be touched kindly. My own mount, Hotspur, nibbled at hay in a desultory fashion as I curried Claire's mare.

"We are not so different, you and I," I said to the horse. "Not so different at all."

When I had finished brushing the mare, I turned to go back into the house, carrying the clothes I had put aside. I didn't even realize I'd left the mask off until I went inside and Maggie saw me. Her sharp intake of breath alerted me to my error, and I sat dejectedly on the hallway settle, clothes dropped next to me and my face in my palms.

"I am so sorry," I whispered. "I never wanted you to see."

"Mister LeMaitre," she replied, "I won't think another thing of it. You're that worried about the mistress, aren't you, if you didn't remember?"

Gilbert and Honor came downstairs then, and my valet seemed surprised to see me barefaced as well. It was my great shame that tears began to flow at that point; I could not recall ever feeling so completely bereft. Even Christine's betrayal had not hurt like this.

Honor brushed past Gilbert and put her arms around me.

"There, there, sir. The mistress will be fine. Just you wait and see."

It was the most the girl had ever said to me, and somehow that increased the pain. What other woman would give as much to me as Claire had done?

At London Hospital, in Whitechapel, Dr. Treves deposited me at what I presumed was his surgery office door.

"I'm wanted in the operating theatre, Madame LeMaitre. Please make yourself at home," he said. He bowed to me and left me alone.

I let myself into the suite, but saw no one. From a back room came a muffled "I shall be with you in a moment. Please have a seat."

"Thank you, I shall," I responded.

"Oh, my goodness. A lady caller? I wish I had known. I would have rung for tea." From out of the back room came the man to whom the muffled voice belonged. The reason for his tone was immediately obvious: his mouth and head were grossly malformed, as was one side of his body. However, the hand he extended to me was as beautiful and graceful as a woman's.

"Madame, please allow me to introduce myself. I am Joseph

Merrick. Sir Frederick isn't here just now. May I have the sisters bring you tea?"

I wracked my brain, for Merrick's name was familiar to me. I finally remembered reading an article in the London Times about him: the press called him "the Elephant Man."

I took the hand extended to me and sketched a brief curtsey.

"Thank you, Monsieur Merrick. Tea would be lovely. I am Madame Claire LeMaitre."

I took the proffered chair and continued. "Monsieur Merrick, Doctor Treves asked me to wait for him here. I believe that he wanted me to visit a patient."

"Perhaps it was I whom he wished you to see? Sir Frederick had said he would try to arrange callers for me. I am rather lonely here. And please, could you call me Joseph?"

"But of course. And I am Claire. So, you are Doctor Treves' patient?"

"Yes, and his friend. Sir Frederick rescued me from a traveling circus and I have lived here at London Hospital since then; he is trying to learn about my disease."

I understood then how the doctor thought I could help. Erik's face was not even a patch on what poor Joseph's case, to be sure. I was unafraid of what many people found freakish and frightening. How many women would take tea with Joseph Merrick?

"I see. Well, in a way I do anyway. I am not a nurse, Joseph. How am I to help you?"

"Claire, your presence is a help. I long to be able to take tea, or to discuss a book I have read. These simple pleasures happen but rarely."

I sighed. How well I knew that refrain; it had not been that long since Erik himself had been in the same position.

The young sister who brought the tea service was evidently nervous about the proposition. I took the tray from her and sent her on her way with an assurance that all was well.

"Shall I pour out, Joseph?"

"That would be very kind of you."

I took the opportunity to study Merrick further while I arranged the tea things. His suit was of good quality, though it fit poorly; I assumed from this that his body was as malformed as his unfortunate head. Unlike Erik, Joseph could do nothing to hide his deformity and so it was there for the world to see and jeer at. The cruelty of humanity never ceased to amaze me.

Merrick arranged a napkin in his shirt collar. I wondered at this breech of etiquette in the otherwise gently mannered soul until he took his first swallow of tea; his misshapen mouth was unable to contain the beverage and it thus spilled everywhere. I had a brief memory of Philippe; after the fire, he had been much the same and very ashamed of it. Merrick seemed either not to care or to have accepted the mess as a natural course of events. I opted to do the same.

"So, Joseph, how is it that you came to be in Doctor Treves' care?"

"He found me caged in the circus," Joseph began.

My eyes widened and my hands shook so that I could no longer hold my saucer. I sat down my tea things. The image of Erik, captured and caged by my cousin, was still very fresh in my mind.

"Claire, are you all right?" Joseph inquired. "Is the tea too strong for you?"

"No, Joseph. I assure you. I am fine." My hands, twisting the corner of my napkin, belied my words, but I asked him to continue his story.

It paralleled Erik's in so many ways that it brought tears to my eyes. The assumption that his malformity had rendered him impervious to insult: the beatings, the humiliation. Finally, Treves had purchased Merrick from the showman and brought him to London, where he now lived in apartments behind the surgery on Bedstead Square.

"Sir Frederick has given me a new life, you see," Joseph continued. "He hopes to find a cure for my malady. He brings me books and newspapers to read so that I may keep up on current events. I enjoy reading, and knowing what is happening in the world. My favorite book is the Bible, and I have read it several times. I do long to go to the opera or the theatre like other gentlemen but, alas, that is not to be. But I have met the Princess Alexandra. She is my friend."

So much like Erik, I thought. It was then that Treves's intent became clear to me.

"Joseph, I may be able to arrange to call on you now and again. Would you like that?"

He looked briefly at my left hand, marking the ring I wore. "Madame, what would your husband think of you passing time with another gentleman?"

"She'd be better chaperoned than this, Joseph," a voice behind me said. "No, Madame LeMaitre there is no need to stand. Joseph, you should have asked one of the sisters to remain with you." Dr. Treves' tone was gentle yet remonstrative.

"Shall I ring for more cups?" Merrick inquired. "Claire and I are having a lovely tea."

"It is time for Claire to be going, Joseph. I will be taking her home now."

I was surprised at how quickly the time had flown.

"Thank you, Monsieur Merrick, for the tea." I had enjoyed his company, and said so.

"You will come again?" he asked, as he stood. Merrick's manners were impeccable.

"If Doctor Treves will allow it," I responded as I donned my shawl and bonnet. I made to leave, but then turned around.

"Monsieur Merrick, you are missing something in your lovely home. There is no tray for me to leave a card showing that I am at home to you."

"Is that how it is done in most homes, Claire?"

I nodded my assent as I took a card from my reticule and extended it to him.

"I shall have Mrs. Mothershead, the directress of the sisters, arrange for a tray at once," he responded with dignity as he accepted the little parchment rectangle. "Thank you for your kindness."

CHAPTER 41

In the carriage, I had a lengthy conversation with Doctor Treves about visiting Joseph on a regular basis. We reached an agreement whereby I would come occasionally to play cards or share books with his patient.

When we arrived at my home, Erik and Gilbert were deep in conversation. After saying my farewells to Doctor Treves, Erik asked Gilbert to excuse us. We were alone.

From the pages of Erik's journal:

My conversation with Claire that afternoon was most enlightening. While Gilbert had told me that she was unhappy playing the lady of leisure, I had no idea how deeply entrenched that feeling had become.

However, there was some tension. When Claire told me she had spent the afternoon visiting with Joseph Merrick, whose name was known to me through the newspapers, and that she intended to do so again, I could not contain my outburst.

"Is it your intent, Claire, to collect every broken creature and sideshow freak on the planet?"

I wished I could take back the words as soon as I saw the injured look on her face. Her kindness to both Rochambeau and me was not a thing to throw up in an argument, and yet that was just what I had done.

"You, of all people, should know the answer to that," she said quietly as she stood and made her way toward the staircase.

"Oh, God, Claire. I am so sorry."

Her hand on the newel post, she turned to face me.

"Are you, Erik? Christine, after all, would not want to spend her time tending to an injured horse, or a rescued cat or, god help her, yet another beautiful soul who has been mistreated because of a misshapen body." A single tear coursed down her cheek. "I can never live up to what she would do, Erik. I can only be who I am."

"Is that what all of this is about?" I was astonished.

"No, Erik, it's only part of it. I feel useless. Stultified. I'm trying to do the right things, be the right kind of wife for a man of your position. And then, I see how you looked at that girl. I'm not stupid, Erik. I know you still love her."

She turned and mounted the stairwell. I spoke softly to her retreating back, but I knew she would hear.

"Claire, you couldn't be more wrong."

She turned and looked down to where I stood.

"Am I?"

"Am I?"

The words hung in the air between us. My tone betrayed my exhaustion, misery and depression as well as an overt challenge. When Erik said nothing, I made my way upstairs to my room once more. I almost turned around, but decided that I couldn't bear to see the pity in Erik's eyes: pity for the woman whom he had not loved so well as he thought.

"Claire," he whispered, laying a hand on my shoulder.

I started; his habit of moving in catlike silence had never changed and he'd come up behind me quickly. I turned to face him. He was standing on the next riser down from me, which reduced the disparity in our heights. His anguish showed in the emerald gaze he turned toward me.

"I don't know what else I can do but to tell you, Claire." His voice was just as quiet and defeated as mine had been moments before. "After that, I can only ask that you believe me."

I didn't know what to say, so I remained silent for a moment, gathering my thoughts.

"Erik, I ..."

My words were silenced by a kiss that was both tender and passionate. His lips were gentle and firm and, as always, I melted at his touch.

"I need you, Claire," he whispered afterward. "I love you."

"I promised Monsieur Merrick that I would call upon him again, Erik." My tone was slightly less defiant but firm nonetheless.

"Very well, then," Erik responded. "I will have Michael take you to the hospital."

I agreed to the plan, asking to be taken to London Hospital around three o'clock the next day. That would allow for a pleasant visit with my new acquaintance.

Erik pressed his lips to the back of my hand. "Of course, Claire. Whatever will help."

I was about to go upstairs when the bell rang. Erik himself opened the door to admit Lady Alice Harrington, who sailed past him without a by-your-leave.

"Claire, you and I must talk. I was here earlier and your butler said you'd been taken to hospital."

"I had a doctor's appointment," I replied. I figured it was none of her business why I had been there. I gestured toward the parlor, and Alice made herself at home.

"We must speak Claire. Your behavior is reprehensible. You are never 'at home' to company. You prefer the company of animals and ... servants ... to women of your own station. You don't call on others who have left cards on you. It's scandalous, Claire; the other ladies have remarked on it. And now, Lady Anne Treves tells me you spent the afternoon in the company of some circus freak of her husband's. You need to think about Erik's position and keep to your place."

I lashed out, no longer able to contain my fury.

"Alice, I find cold comfort in the idea that someone claiming to be my friend would allow me to become fodder for idle gossip. The ladies who leave cards on me do not leave their addresses. You are the only one to whom I am at home, and I believe it is only so that you can carry new gossip to the others."

"You see?" Alice continued placidly. "You are so ... French. Good English women would never put themselves in a position to provoke gossip. It appears to be a French habit, though. For goodness' sake, the Vicomtesse de Chagny doesn't even have the decency to go into confinement ... showing off her condition in society." She made a disapproving moue.

I was appalled, to say the least, and could not muster a response. Beyond appalled, I was hurt by what I saw as my friend's betrayal.

"I wouldn't want to embarrass you any further," I whispered. "Perhaps it is best if you go."

"I'm sorry, Claire. I thought it best that you knew." She rose then and left our home, without bothering to leave a card in the salver.

I slept alone again that night. Erik did not tell me where he spent his nights, and I was too bereft to care. I wanted real friends, friends who spoke my language and did not mock me behind my back. It seemed such a simple thing, and yet it was not to be. The only French voices I heard were Erik and Gilbert, and it was not enough. At the same time, I had to try harder to fit in for Erik's sake. I fell asleep with my arms around the toy Josephine, planning how I would be a better wife.

CHAPTER 42

Now I had told Erik how I felt about my lot, and he did not say a word one way or the other. I thus had no idea whether he was in agreement with the concerns I expressed. All I knew was that I was miserable. The whole thing made me ineffably sad.

I saw Erik as being part of the same social class as any landed gentry. His investments meant that he need not keep an office in someone else's firm. Yet, I had not thought of how I fit into that particular picture. I could only try to undo whatever damage I had unwittingly caused.

I gathered up a deck of cards and some books for Joseph Merrick; Michael Stubbins took me to London Hospital in our little coach. Merrick and I could play a hand or two of some game and talk for a while before Michael collected me. After getting directions from two different sisters, I made my way to Joseph Merrick's rooms once again. I knocked at the door and let myself in.

"Doctor Treves? Monsieur Merrick?" I called quietly.

"One moment," came Merrick's muffled voice from the small back room. He emerged whilst adjusting his necktie.

"Oh! Madame LeMaitre! I am so glad you have come to visit again. Sir Frederick is lecturing just now."

"Please, Joseph. We had agreed that you were to call me Claire," I smiled. "I brought you some gifts." I proffered the parcel to him.

"This really is too kind," Joseph demurred as he unwrapped the books and cards. "Sir Frederick's friends are too generous to me. Just last night, Mrs. Kendall brought me the loveliest fitted travel case. Do you know Mrs. Kendall? She is an actress."

I shook my head "no," and Merrick continued.

"Sir Frederick brought her to visit yesterday evening. I never thought that I would have such beautiful lady callers as you and Mrs. Kendall. She left her photograph for me as well. Shall I ring for tea?"

Merrick seemed particularly excited today, I thought, as he jumped from subject to subject.

"Tea would be very nice, thank you."

Merrick rang for a sister and made his needs known: "The nice cups today, if you please, Nora. As you can see, I have a guest and we really must not stint in these situations."

When the young nurse departed, Joseph asked if I wanted to play whist. I had to confess that I did not know the game, nor did Merrick know the ones with which I was familiar.

"Very well, then, let us just chat," he said as another sister brought in the tea tray. "Thank you, Sister. Claire, would you pour out, please?"

I poured the steaming liquid into delicate porcelain cups painted with violets; Nora had taken Joseph at his word.

I had planned to make small-talk: to pretend that I was at Alice Harrington's at-home day and talk about the weather and such. I wanted to practice so that I would make no more of my ignorant French mistakes. Instead, I found myself telling Joseph everything that had transpired, beginning with the opera gala and culminating in Lady Harrington's visit the day before.

Merrick remained silent for a moment and then placed his empty cup and saucer on the tray. Once again, I could not help but mark the contrast between his graceful hand and his misshapen face.

"Claire," he spoke at last, "'Men like your husband and me really want only one thing: to be accepted by society. Erik enjoys the advantage of having a wife. I, on the other hand, despair of being loved by a woman."

"You too, Joseph? Does no one think I am capable of doing right?"

Joseph handed me his handkerchief, for I had started to cry.

"I never say things correctly," he sighed. "I wish I had a wife to be gossiped over: someone who loves me for myself and doesn't care about the mortal shell. Do you know how I envy your Erik? I have even asked Doctor Treves if he might find a place for me at a hospital for the blind. That way, perhaps a woman would love me without having to look at my face."

I tried very hard to calm myself, but I failed miserably.

"Claire, please don't cry." Merrick moved to sit next to me on the settee and was patting my hand gently (I was sure he had read somewhere that this was comforting) when Erik walked into the room.

"Monsieur Merrick, I presume?" Erik sketched a bow as Merrick stood. "I see that you have met my wife already."

"Erik," I sniffled as I folded Joseph's handkerchief, "This is Joseph Merrick. Monsieur Merrick, I will have your kerchief laundered and returned to you."

Erik and Joseph sized one another up for a brief silent period. Then, with a graceful gesture, Erik removed his mask.

"She understands us very well, doesn't she?" he said quietly before covering his ravaged face again.

"Yes, Monsieur LeMaitre," Joseph said. "I can only hope to be as blessed as you one day. She loves you very much."

Erik nodded. "If you want her to come again, I will arrange for it."

Every inch of me wanted to cry out that I could speak for myself. Instead, I remained silent.

"I will send an invitation around, if that's all right," Merrick said. "Perhaps, the next time, you will both come and we can teach Madame LeMaitre to play whist. And, Madame, I would be honored if you would bring me a photograph to add to my mantle. Doctor Treves tells me that people display photographs of their friends and family there."

We said our goodbyes then, and Erik and I went through the corridors to the waiting gig.

"I thought to surprise you by collecting you myself," Erik said as he helped me to the seat. He flicked the reins across Blackjack's patient haunches and we trotted smartly through town back toward our home.

I was seated to Erik's right; the mask hid much of his expression. He was freshly shaven and barbered and his clothing, as always, was immaculate. Gilbert had proved to be the perfect valet for my fastidious husband. It was all I could do to keep my hands folded daintily in my lap. My strongest impulse was to caress Erik's well-muscled thigh in a manner that could only be a prelude to lovemaking. However, I suspected that proper English ladies did not do such things at all, let alone in open carriages. I wanted desperately to do the right thing by my husband.

"You are uncharacteristically quiet, Claire," he finally remarked, his tone neutral. "Perhaps you would like to tell me why? Or did you manage to get it all out of your system whilst crying in Monsieur

Merrick's arms?"

Once again, I found myself relating my discussions with Lady Harrington. I rambled on about visiting cards, and at-home days ... and realized that I was not making much sense.

Finally, I just blurted it out. "I will try, Erik. I will do everything I can to be the right kind of wife for a man of your position. But it won't be easy for me."

Erik was silent, so I continued.

"You know I wasn't born to this. I'm not Olympia Harrington, with a dragon-like mama teaching me every move to make. Nor am I Alice Harrington, who is good at sitting about and doing little but gossip. But, I will try."

This last came as Erik pulled the gig into our cobblestoned stable yard. Michael was there to take Blackjack's reins.

"Once the horses are cared for, I want you go go home to Maggie and your children, Michael. I don't want to see any of you for the next three days. Madame needs the quiet to recover."

"Yes, sir," Michael replied.

I nodded, wondering what my husband was about, as the two of us went into the house.

"Just what is it that you think I want in a wife?" Erik whispered, bending down so that his warm breath caressed my ear.

He brushed his lips across my forehead.

"Go upstairs. I'll join you momentarily." His green eyes were dark with unmistakable desire.

I wrapped my arms around his neck and drew him closer for a kiss.

"I'll be waiting," I whispered back, and then went upstairs, unpinning my bonnet as I went. This was, no doubt, another deplorable habit. Just then, I didn't care.

CHAPTER 43

January-February 1890

From the pages of Erik's journal:

Those days alone, even though the Stubbins family was just across the yard in their home above the carriage house, were a tonic to Claire and me both. She shed the air of melancholia that had hung about her since the opera gala. Her demeanor was gay as she played with Pierre or worked with Angel in the yard.

And, oh, when we made love. Words cannot express how profoundly beautiful it was to be in her embrace, tasting her kisses and drinking in the warm scent of her skin.

Gilbert and Honor used one of those free days to visit Gretna Green and were married. Claire and Maggie prepared a wedding supper for them, and we all sat together in the large dining room. When Honor expressed her concerns about the propriety of servants eating with the family, Claire silenced her with a laugh.

"Honor, my dear, we are *en famille*: with our family. You are my friends, you know." She presented Honor with a beautifully embroidered shawl, and gave Gilbert a handsome walking stick with a blue glass ball for a handle.

I was very happy, and it seemed that Claire's fears about her place in society had ebbed. She occasionally went on calls with Madame Harrington, leaving cards on the society matrons. Her friendship with that lady had cooled considerably, but Claire made every possible effort to fit in with polite society.

As the weeks wore on, I watched Claire grow sad again. On yet another at-home day when no one came to call, I found her in tears in the parlor.

"Erik, why?" she sobbed. "I have tried so hard. I have gone to the other ladies' homes; I have paid my calls. I have tried to talk about books, and the plays or ballet. But they just shut me out."

Having been an immigrant myself so many times, I understood what Claire did not. Despite my previous reticence, I found myself telling her about traveling around Europe, living in Russia and Persia, and how I had been outcast not only because of my face but because I did not know the customs of those around me. I understood that it has ever been thus for those who uproot themselves and dare to brave a new life. Claire had never experienced the cutting unkindness to which I was almost immune after enduring it for a lifetime.

"Your ways are foreign to them," I finished, "and, because they have not seen so much of the world, are frightening."

Claire shook her head in astonishment. "What can be frightening about expanding your mind and horizons?"

"My treasure," I responded, brushing my lips across her forehead, "small minds fear the unknown."

It was some weeks since I had last bothered to hold an at-home day. The air was was ripe with scents of early spring, and I donned breeches, boots and a roll-necked pullover to work with Angel in the stable yard. She had gained weight, muscling out beautifully, and her coat bloomed with dapples. Michael's and my gentle ministrations had paid off with the high-strung mare. She bugled whenever she saw me approaching her stall; the peppermint puffs in my pocket didn't hurt matters.

I saddled Angel and positioned her near the mounting block. This would be my first attempt at actually riding the mare after several weeks with Michael or me working her on a long rein to build up her strength, and I didn't know what to expect. Michael held my stirrup as I swung my leg over; I loathed the sidesaddle and refused to bother any further with it.

Angel snorted as I settled my weight onto her back, but didn't budge.

"Michael, if you'd be so kind as to lead her around the yard?" I requested. "I just want her to get accustomed to the idea of being ridden again."

A few circuits of the yard and I was confident that the mare would cooperate with me. Not only did she have a delicate, elastic step, but she collected beautifully, tucking her head down to get on the bit and shortening her steps. Erik stepped outside to the mews as I asked Angel for a collected trot; the mare's gait floated her across the yard.

"She was someone's very well-trained pet once, I suspect," Erik pronounced as I dismounted and turned the mare over to Michael to cool. She was not yet fit enough for long rides and I didn't want to push her endurance.

"Indeed. Perhaps one day soon, you and I will take these beautiful animals for a ride up Rotten Row. I can only imagine the scandalized looks at my breeches," I laughed. I had more than once remarked on my amazement that the English would call Rue de Roi, "street of the king," Rotten Row; however, it was a favorite hacking spot for those who kept horses in town.

"I cannot tell you how it pleases me to hear your laughter, Claire." He caressed my cheek, tipping my chin up for a kiss. His hands were astonishingly cold, and I remarked on that.

"It happens in the winter, and it has ever been thus," he shrugged, coughing a little at the same time. I made a mental note to see the glover on his behalf; clearly the fine kid gloves Erik favored would have to be lined for colder weather. If I had understood how damp and chill London winters could be, I would have arranged for it sooner.

"Come inside, Claire, and let us warm ourselves," Erik said, putting an arm around my shoulders. "I need to talk with you."

"You sound so solemn, Erik. What is it?"

"I have decided to take on Olympia Harrington as my pupil," he said as we went indoors. "I hope that it will help you to be accepted if we make this overture."

"But, Erik," I protested, "You said you didn't want to take a student, let alone Olympia."

"I do not," he rejoined. "However, a conciliatory gesture toward Olympia is also a gesture toward her mother. I cannot like how you are shut out of the ladies' activities."

"You do not understand, Erik," I sighed as I headed upstairs to change my clothes. "I don't think I want to be like those ladies at all."

"Perhaps not, Claire," he called after me. "But you cannot live always in isolation. I know this for certain. You need the goodwill of those women, whether you like it or not."

I shook my head sadly and went into the bedroom. He was probably correct.

My greatest fear had nothing to do with the society matrons at all. It was that the last student he had taken was Christine Daae ... and he was in love with her. Could it be that there was more to his decision that met the eye? The Honorable Olympia was, after all, a graceful beauty with perfect English manners.

Would I never feel secure in my marriage? Some days I wondered. At least Erik was spending his nights at home again. He no longer resorted to the opium dens of Limehouse; he had finally confessed to me what he had been about.

CHAPTER 44

April 1890

It was early April, and the spring flowers were blooming. The weather even warmed up a little. Erik had just sent Olympia on her way after another lesson; under his tutelage, she was making progress as a singer. Perhaps she would achieve her ambition of singing at Covent Garden after all. I was in the kitchen with Maggie, helping peel vegetables for supper. Erik came in to get a cup of tea; Olympia's lessons usually ended with him coughing painfully and the hot drink soothed his throat.

"Erik, perhaps you should see a doctor," I said. "That cough has been nagging at you for nearly three weeks."

"It's nothing, Claire. Just a spring cold; it will clear up before long, I am sure." He leaned down to kiss my forehead. "I'm going to read for a while, my dear. And don't you worry about me. Everything will be fine."

I sighed in resignation. My husband was a very stubborn man. At least we were both keeping busy in our own ways.

I had visited Joseph Merrick several more times over the past few weeks, and we were becoming fast friends. He confided to me that he was venturing out of his little rooms at Bedstead Square more often and that people made an effort to shake his hand.

"Of course, I must wear my cap, hood and cloak; I would not want to frighten the ladies who do not know me," he said ruefully.

"But nevertheless it is good to be about the town."

He showed me a beautiful replica of St. Philip's cathedral, built out of cardboard, that he had made himself.

"I can only see the spire," he said, indicating the view out of his basement window, "so the rest is my imagination. But I am quite pleased with it. Doctor Treves has promised to send it to Princess Alexandra for me. Do you think she will like it?"

I responded that I was sure Her Highness would be quite grateful to receive such a lovely gift.

"Is that her picture there, Joseph?" I indicated the photograph on his mantle, in a place of prominence between my photograph and Mrs. Kendall's.

"Yes, it is. She sent it along for me. What a kind woman she is. Society ladies are so nice to me." Joseph was so very pleased during that visit, the delight palpable in his voice and demeanor.

I only wished that they were so nice to everyone. I had to admit that Erik's plan to tutor Olympia Harrington had helped me gain entree into the ladies' good graces again. However, I still found them dull and preferred the company of my own little circle at home. Even Honor had warmed up to me now that she and Gilbert were wed.

Dolly came into the kitchen then, carrying her schoolbooks and looking rather forlorn.

"Good evening, Ma'am Claire," she said to me. "Good evening, Mummy."

"Why the long face, miss," Maggie asked. "You look as though you lost your best friend."

"It isn't that at all, Mummy. I just wish I didn't have to go to school anymore."

"Dolly," I said as I put the vegetables aside, "Your education is very important. It's a wonderful thing that Prince Albert created so many public schools so that everyone can learn. You're very fortunate."

"Oh, no, Ma'am Claire. It isn't that at all. I love to learn things; I just don't want to go to school anymore. I do not like the children there; they say mean things."

"Like what," Maggie sat down and looked her daughter in the eye. "Tell me what's the matter."

"What is a hoor, mother?" The child was solemn. "One of the little girls at school said Ma'am Claire was a hoor: that all French ladies are hoors."

"Oh, god in heaven," I sighed.

"Dorothy," Maggie replied sternly, "Those are not the sorts of discussions we should be having. Nice young ladies do not use those words."

"But what is it, Mummy? The way that girl talked about Ma'am Claire made it sound like it was very bad."

"Who is this girl, Dolly?" I asked.

"Her mummy does for the Harringtons. She said Miss Olympia said you were a hoor and that 'Sieur Erik should find a proper lady."

Erik entered the kitchen just then for another cup of tea.

"What on earth are we talking about?" he asked.

"Mummy and Ma'am Claire will not tell me what a hoor is," Dolly pronounced seriously.

"Well, Madamoiselle Dolly, a whore is a woman who lies with a man for money and presents," Erik replied.

"Hmm," the girl mused. "Ma'am Claire doesn't do that."

"No," I replied, "I do not."

"But that means Miss Olympia is a hoor," Dolly announced.

Erik's laughter was rich and throaty, and I am afraid to say that I joined in. Maggie sent Dolly out to the family quarters above the stables to do her lessons; she was having too much trouble stifling her amusement.

Dinner was on the table when a knock came at the door. Jamie answered it, and came to tell us that a cab man was there. Erik went to see what was the matter, and returned shortly with Joseph Merrick.

"I am sorry to interrupt your evening, Claire," he said. "I believed this would be your at-home day and I thought I would call."

"Joseph, I am so delighted to see you. Let Erik help you off with your wraps and perhaps you will join us for dinner." I smiled in welcome. "I was just thinking about our last visit and am so glad you have come."

"I would not want to put you out," Joseph rejoined.

"Not at all. We have plenty," I said. "We are taking dinner in the kitchen this evening, as a family."

Erik helped Joseph off with his cap, cloak and hood, and we all went into the kitchen. Maggie and Dolly gasped, and Honor looked down at her plate. Gilbert, on the other hand, stood to greet our guest and introduced himself.

"Let me assist you, Mister Merrick. Madame Claire has told us so much about you. I am delighted to make your acquaintance."

Gilbert could always be counted upon for an unflappable response, and the others fortunately took their cue from him.

"Yes, Mister Merrick. Let me make you a plate," Maggie said. She went to the stove to prepare another setting.

"You did not tell me you had such a large family, Claire," Joseph said.

"We're the staff," Gilbert replied. "Erik and Claire treat us like family. Please permit me to make the introductions."

I was grateful to Gilbert and Erik that night for their kindness toward my friend. He had taken an enormous risk in leaving his safe little home to see me.

We ate our meal amidst discussion of books and plays. It reminded me of the old days in Paris, when we would all talk about the news of the day. It was one of the nicest evenings I had passed in a long while and I said as much to Joseph when Michael helped him into our little coach to take him home.

"I shall come and see you tomorrow, Joseph. I am so glad you came tonight. Sleep well, *mon ami*." I waved good-bye to the little coach and went back inside.

Unfortunately, it was the last time that I would see my friend; I learned from Doctor Treves the next day that Joseph had died in his sleep. He was accustomed to sleep sitting up, surrounded by pillows, but that particular night he had slept lying down and asphyxiated due to the weight of his head. I was devasted by the news.

"When will the funeral take place, Frederick?" I asked as I dried my tears.

"There won't be a funeral, Claire. I have arranged for castings to be made of Joseph's body. An anatomist is going to preserve the skeleton for me."

I was appalled. Joseph had been a devout Christian; he often told me that his favorite reading material was the Bible. Regardless of my own rather un-churched ways, I did not think that this was right at all and said so.

"I am sorry you feel that way, Claire," Treves rejoined. "Joseph Merrick will make an enormous contribution to the sciences this way, and that is far more important than religious superstition. I hope that your husband will consider that when his own time comes."

I was too shocked at the doctor's temerity to respond and so I walked away. I wondered whether Treves had really cared about Erik or me at all. Once he saw Erik's face unmasked, I suspected, he was already planning for his next curiosity presentation at the hospital's rounds. It made me angry to even think about it.

But there was also nothing I could do. I made my way home and shared the sad news with our household.

"None of us will forget him, Claire," Erik said. "We will all remember Joseph in our own way."

We would have spoken further, but Olympia arrived for her singing lesson. Gilbert followed me upstairs.

"Is there anything I can do, Claire?"

I shook my head. "I just need to be by myself right now, Gilbert. I could not have imagined the world could be so cruel."

He closed the door behind himself, and I listened to his halting footsteps on the stairs.

CHAPTER 45

May-June 1890

From the pages of Erik's journal:

My cough is growing steadily worse, and today there was blood on my handkerchief. Claire persuaded me to see a doctor at London Hospital, and he told me that there is dampness in my lungs. That I need a warmer climate.

I am reluctant to uproot Claire again. Merrick's death affected her greatly, all the moreso because of how his earthly remains were dealt with. She tried discussing her feelings with the ladies who came to her at-home (yes, at long last), but they did not understand.

"How could you care about a circus freak, Claire," Alice Harrington asked her. "It's not as though he was a person of quality."

How shocked that lady would be if her daughter ever saw the maestro's unmasked face. I am no longer providing instruction to Olympia, for she is now *enceinte* and has laid the pregnancy at the door of a local burgess. A rather hurried wedding is in the offing, I am told.

I must write to Zareh and ask him to complete a single task so that I can return to France. It is time for us to go home, I think. To the south of France this time, to Provence or Camargue, so that I will have the warmer climate the doctor ordered and Claire will have peace of mind.

I fussed over Erik more than I ought to have done, I am sure. He could hardly move without me bringing him a soothing linctus or a hot drink. I was afraid of losing him to the catarrh in his chest; on the heels of Merrick's death, I would doubtless become unhinged.

Erik's ailment also gave me a good excuse to stop my at-home days for the foreseeable future; I had no more stomach for Alice Harrington's society. When I was not nursing my husband, I was riding one of the horses.

Sometimes Erik insisted that Gilbert take me to a museum so that I would get out of the house for a while and he could work on his correspondence with Zareh. Another move was in the offing, this one at the doctor's orders, and I would be happy to close up the house. I wrote references for the entire Stubbins family and had no doubt that they would find situations when we were ready to leave. I planned to give them some money to help make the transition easier, even though I was told it was unnecessary. I could not just leave these kindly people without support while they sought other benefactors. Gilbert and Honor found a flat in town to rent, and established their own household. Doctor Treves arranged to make Gilbert his valet; they would be well provided for.

It was almost June when Erik received a parcel from Zareh. In it were a deed to a farm just outside Avignon, and a copy of *Le Matin*. In the newspaper was an agony item that read "Erik is dead." It was these items that Erik had been waiting to receive.

He sat in a chair in front of the fireplace, where he could be kept warm and comfortable. He seldom wore his mask anymore; the coughing fits dislodged it anyway and there was no one to see him except our family of friends. He hated being treated like an invalid, but tolerated my fussing.

"I told Christine Daae that I would have Zareh place this item in the paper when I was gone," Erik explained. "She will tell the Opera Garnier folk, and word will reach the authorities. No one will look for me again. Everyone will believe I am dead."

I shuddered; the English have a saying about geese walking over one's grave, and this was what they meant.

"Please, Erik, don't talk of your death even in jest. Let us just arrange to be gone from this place. We are going home, my love, and everything will be fine. I will make sure of it."

"Don't tempt the gods, Claire," Erik whispered, and I leaned over so that he could kiss me. "I love you. Never forget that you healed me."

"My darling, please don't be so melancholy," I begged. "All will be well once we are back in France."

He coughed again as I knelt down and put my head in his lap. "I hope you're right," he sighed.

CHAPTER 46

Avignon, France
April 1895

I laid the freshly cut roses on Erik's grave.

"Come, Veronique."

I extended my hand to our daughter. She was nearly five years old, and possessed not only of Erik's jet-black hair but also his rather solemn demeanor. Even at her young age, she preferred the company of books and animals to that of children; in that regard, she took after me.

"Maman, I do not see why we cannot go to the circus," she complained as I boosted her up into the caleche. She could see the tents in the distance and was curious about them.

I stepped into the little coach and took up the reins, flicking them gently across Josephine's back. She trotted off smartly, leaving the hilltop cemetery behind.

"I told you, my dear. They do unkind things to people in those shows."

She pouted a little, her green eyes flashing just as her father's used to do. "It's not fair, Maman."

"No, my child, I suppose it is not. But that is the way of things. When you are a grown lady, you may choose to visit the circus. For now, I will choose that you not."

I pulled the coach up behind our *mas*, a Provençal farmhouse.

Just as I had always wished, it had terra cotta plastered walls and blue shutters to protect against the mistral winds. It was sunny and beautiful in Avignon; I planned never to leave. The modest house was like a palace to me. I loved each room, from the chambers with their iron bedsteads and boutis quilts to the colorfully tiled kitchen with its simple furnishings and plain dishes. This was, at last, truly a home for me.

Veronique and I lived alone. Even the Provençal sun had not been able to stop the dampness in Erik's lungs; we had not left England soon enough to keep the pleurisy at bay. Toward the end of his life, he was bedridden and coughing blood: his beautiful voice was ruined. Veronique was not quite four years old when her father died. One day I would let her read his journals, the which I treasured. Despite the cruelty he had inflicted on me more than once, I loved him and cared for him until the end of his days.

I was grateful that he had died in France, where Zareh helped me to arrange a proper funeral and burial. The idea of Erik's remains suffering the humiliation of an anatomist's knife was more than I could bear. I still missed Joseph Merrick, and it pained me that Doctor Treves cared more about making a name for himself than about the gentle soul he had exploited toward that end.

I unharnessed Josephine and brushed her before turning her out into the pasture. Hotspur, Angel and Cesare were grazing there already, and she galloped out to meet her companions. Ours was a happy little estate.

"Maman," Veronique slipped up behind me; she had also inherited her father's stealth. "May I see if Elise has had her kittens?"

"Yes, my dear, but be careful. She may not want you there if she has babies."

"No, Maman. She will let me. And yes, I know to keep Pierre away." I had already taught her that father cats sometimes kill their own offspring and that my spoiled house cat would be no exception.

I sighed as I watched my black-clad daughter head off to the garden shed where the little calico had made her nest. I still did not believe in the custom of mourning garb, but it had its uses. When Erik's will was read, leaving me the entirety of his substantial fortune, I was grateful for the black weeds that held off potential suitors. I had no male guardian, and so was considered ripe spoils for the taking.

It seemed that every Provençal man, truffle hunter or burgess, was determined to pay court ("after a decent interval, of course, Madame") to the Widow LeMaitre. Dressing my daughter and myself in black was like donning armor. None of the Provençal men had a hope of turning my head anyway; Erik had spoiled me to the point that only someone truly special would do when I was ready for courting again. And that day, I had long since admitted to myself, was unlikely ever to come.

It had been a lonely time without him, though. Sometimes I would look back on the short time we had together, amazed at what we had packed into those few years. He gave me the home I had always wanted, as well as financial independence that most French women would never see. I could travel freely, and all of our holdings were in my name alone. Zareh administered the funds for me from his Paris home, and I lacked for nothing.

I went into the house and took off my coal-scuttle bonnet. I changed out of my plain black dress into a lavender calico frock; the lighter fabric was so much more comfortable as the days grew warmer, and Erik always loved to see me in that color. I sighed, remembering the simple flannel night rail he had bought for me on our wedding trip; Erik had always known what looked best on me.

It was the hottest time of the afternoon. For tea, I planned to prepare a simple snack for Veronique and myself: saucissons and brioches with hot chocolate. I would make her supper later. As for me, I had never fully recovered from one aspect of the melancholia that struck me in London: I still ate very little.

Veronique came in and sat down on the settle near the fireplace.

"Still no kittens, Maman." She was obviously disappointed.

"They will come in their own time, my sweet. Now, play your violin lesson for me."

The tune that Veronique's instructor had taught her was a simple one, and she performed it nicely for me. She put down the instrument, and sighed.

"I wish Papa were still here to play for us, Maman."

"I do, too. But he is with the angels now."

"Is it true that some people thought he was the Angel of Music?"

"Yes, that is so. And some others thought he was a very bad man indeed."

"Hmm." Veronique got down from the settle and went to look out the window. "Which was he, Maman?"

How on earth could I answer that question? How could I explain Erik's complexities to a child? Angel or devil? In my mind, he had certainly been both at different times.

To buy myself time, I unpinned my hair and sat down next to the hearth to brush it out. After the incident in London I had not cut it again, except for a fashionable fringe across my forehead, and so it was past my waist. I usually kept it tightly braided as I worked around the *mas*, so it rippled as I loosed it

"I am going to sit in the garden for a while, Veronique. You may play indoors if you would like, or you may join me."

"I will play inside, Maman," she said, and got out her dolls. I slipped my feet into a pair of espadrilles, which Erik had called my "peasant shoes," and went out to the garden.

I had created an arbor there, with shady awnings and a comfortable, pillow-covered chaise, for Erik during his last days. I often napped there in the afternoons; it was a good place to think and remember.

Indeed, I fell asleep there that afternoon and was awakened by my daughter.

"Maman, there is a man coming up the walk toward the garden. He doesn't look very tidy." Veronique also had her father's fastidious habits about clothing.

"May the saints preserve me from another Provençal farmer," I sighed as I ran my fingers through my locks to smooth them. "I don't think I can take it today."

"He's not a farmer, Maman. His clothes are too nice, even if they are dusty." She turned to face me. "Besides, I have never seen a farmer who walked with a stick."

"You know that is not so, Veronique. Shepherds use sticks."

"Not like that one, Maman. It is a fancy black one with a blue ball at the top."

It couldn't be, I thought. Surely there were other such walking sticks in the world. This was, no doubt, some stranger whom I could hopefully dismiss so that my daughter and I could have our tea in peace.

"Go inside, my dear," I said. "It would be rude not to lay a place for this gentleman at tea-time." I would deal with this caller as best I could, but he might not take a subtle hint.

I smoothed my skirts and went out to the walkway. As I drew closer, I recognized our visitor and ran down the pavers in my delight to see him.

"Gilbert! Oh, my dear Gilbert!" I would have thrown my arms around him, but there was something uncertain in his demeanor that deterred me. Instead, I came to a halt and waited for him to speak. He had a closely-trimmed Van Dyck beard now, and wore a handsome suit of chocolate brown superfine with a green brocade waistcoat. The ensemble suited his coloring perfectly.

"Hello, Claire." My friend stopped on the cobblestones. "I saw Zareh in Paris, and he told me where you were. I'm sorry about Erik; Zareh also told me about his illness. I lost Honor as well, to the typhoid."

I remembered Maggie's letter telling me the news; I had been so consumed with nursing Erik that I had not written back. I apologized, but he waved my words aside.

"I came to Avignon as soon as I could, hoping to see you. Your home is a bit of a walk from the railroad station and I was unable to hire either a station fly or a horse to bring me here. Could we have a seat? This has been rather a long walk and I would like to rest my leg."

"Oh, my goodness. Of course. You must come in and meet Veronique. She will be so pleased to know one of her father's oldest friends."

"Could we sit down outside for just a moment? I should like to tell you some things first."

"Of course."

I led the way to my shady little arbor. Gilbert took off his jacket and hat, and rolled up his shirtsleeves. His hair was cut fashionably, a bit longer than it had been before, in a tousle of waves untamed by brilliantine. He took a small sketchpad from the pocket of his coat and handed it to me as we sat side-by-side on the chaise.

"Please, have a look. I drew these years ago and have carried them with me."

I opened the notebook and was surprised to see sketch after sketch of me. In some I was on horseback, at the Opera Garnier; I guessed that they were done from memory. The one that most touched me was clearly done in the London house, while I was asleep. My hand was curled under my chin; under it Gilbert had written Shakespeare's words: "Oh, that I were a glove upon that hand."

I looked up at him in confusion.

"They are beautiful sketches," I said quietly. "Why are you showing them to me now?"

"I am an old friend of Veronique's father, but I am more than that." He moved closer to me and put a gentle hand on my waist. "I am also the man who still loves her mother after all of these years."

I looked into Gilbert's warm brown eyes in amazement. His presence alone was testimony to his devotion. Unless he had changed so much that he wanted the money I had inherited. I was crestfallen, and it must have shown in my face.

"Claire, say the word and I'll be gone. I know I took a risk coming here; I even took lodgings in town. My feelings for you have never waned. I also know I'm not good enough for you; you're a wealthy woman and you deserve a gentleman. You deserve far more than I can offer you. But I had to try."

To my surprise, I longed to touch Gilbert's tousled curls more than anything in the world. I reached out a tentative hand and laid it on his cheek.

"My dear, dear Gilbert," I sighed as he lowered his mouth gently to mine, just as he had done once many years before. My fingers entwined in his hair and I began to cry as I let Erik go at last. That chapter in my life was truly closed, even as another opened.

Gilbert held me for a few minutes, his fingers toying with my hair, and murmured endearments. It seemed as though we had always been together; in some ways, we had.

"My darling Claire, we have so much to talk about," he said as he dried my tears with his thumb. "Let us go inside."

Made in the USA
Charleston, SC
06 April 2014